Zandy kept asking herself how Riley Dawson could be so cruel.

"If he had only been kind," Zandy muttered to herself, "I might have actually fallen in love with him."

"What did you say, Zandy?" Ruth leaned over to ask amidst the din of noise.

Zandy shook her head. "Nothing, Ruth." The fact was her statement startled her in a way that she couldn't explain. Was it true? Could she really have thought herself capable of falling in love with Riley Dawson?

She hadn't any time to consider the matter as Riley approached the front of the room.

"If everyone will quiet down, I'll begin this meeting," Riley shouted above the noise. . . .

"I know many of you are unhappy with the new arrangements we've made for your businesses and working hours. I have only one thing to say about the matter. I offered Miss Alexandra Stewart a very tempting proposal, and she rejected me. I suggest if you are unhappy that you take it up with her." Riley stared squarely into Zandy's shocked face. The hurt in her eyes nearly caused him to wince. Why should it bother him that she was upset? He intended to have his own way in this matter and by whatever means it took to accomplish his goal.

The Willing Heart

Janelle Jamison

Heartsong Presents

Dedicated to my husband, Jim. The dream is never so sweet as when shared with someone you love.

ISBN 1-55748-465-1

THE WILLING HEART

PRINTED IN THE U.S.A.

one

Rich ebony darkened the view from peak to peak as if someone had draped black velvet, strewn generously with diamonds, above the mountains of Temperance, Colorado. Alexandra Stewart gazed longingly toward the sky. It reminded her of a luxurious gown she had once seen worn by an opera singer in Kansas City. But that was when her family had lived happily and prosperously in Missouri, not in the mining town of Temperance.

In the distance the church bell was ringing, beckoning the population of the small mountain town to join together on that fateful Sunday night. It was March, 1880, and the town of Temperance was nearly a ghost town. Alexandra, usually called Zandy, was uncertain if she really cared whether the town died or not. Mining towns came and went and, as always its fate followed the ore of the day. These days, silver was booming. Gold was always popular but in Temperance it seemed that neither ore was to be had. With such being the case, the people had exited en masse just as they had come a scant six months ago.

Zandy's father, Burley Stewart, had been one of the masses to give in to tales of striking it rich and living the life of the well-to-do. He'd closed his small dry goods business in Missouri and moved his family to the

5

mountains of Colorado.

The trip had been hard on all of them. They were seven in number on the journey out and, as of last night, they became eight. Ruth Stewart, Zandy's stepmother, had given birth to Molly, and so, after being the only daughter in a mob of wild boys, Zandy had a sister.

"Zandy!" It was her father calling.

"I'm out here, Pa," Zandy called as she made her way into the house. The word "house" was really stretching the definition of this three-room shack but it was the only shelter they could afford, and Zandy had worked hard alongside her stepmother to make it a home.

"Get these boys on down to the church and I'll be along shortly," Burley Stewart directed his daughter. Faithful man that he was, Zandy thought him the best of all possible fathers. The only exception was her Heavenly Father.

"Come on, boys. George, you hold my hand," Zandy said to the smallest boy.

"I'm almost five," George protested, "I don't need anybody holding my hand," he pouted. "I can hold my own hand," and he demonstrated by doing just that.

Zandy couldn't help but laugh and rumple the brown hair of the small boy. "All right, George. You do that." She herded the boys through the thin wooden door and cast a brief glance over her shoulder at her father. "I'll see you at the church," she said and was gone.

The walk wasn't all that far, but the night air was cold and the mountain pathways were slick with ice and snow. Zandy pulled her woolen coat close and soon found George holding up eager arms to be held and kept warm. Zandy lovingly pulled the boy into her arms and snuggled him inside the folds of her coat.

All five were quite grateful to reach the church and walked into the building in total silence. Since they were very small, the children had been raised to respect the house of God. The three older boys were quick to pull their caps off their heads and, with a reverence that seemed almost strange for children, they made their way to the pew. Zandy knew this peacefulness wouldn't last. The boys were, after all, just boys and their attention span was never great.

Zandy took her place beside them, making sure that ten-year-old Joshua was separated from eight-year-old Bart and that George was well within reach to keep him from parading around the church at will. That just left six-year-old Samuel, who was generally less trouble than the rest, and Zandy motioned him to sit beside Bart.

The few people who still lived in Temperance were taking their places in the church. Some waved to Zandy or spoke a brief hello, and soon Burley Stewart joined his children as the minister closed the doors behind him.

Pastor Brokamp made his way to the pulpit and smiled. He was a short, stubby man, with a balding head and a whiskerless face. The lack of a beard or mustache seemed to set him apart as a man of God almost more so than any other feature about him.

"Friends, it's good to see you here tonight," the pastor began. "I must say that I nearly took a spill off Mabel into Meiers Gulch before finally putting my feet on solid ground again." At this the tiny congregation laughed knowing only too well the temperament of the donkey that Pastor Brokamp affectionately called Mabel.

"Nonetheless, I'm here and so are you. I was searching the Word of God last week, seeking to find an appropriate verse to teach on and the Lord bestowed a beautiful passage upon my heart."

"Did God talk to Pastor Brokamp?" George asked his father in a loud whisper.

"I reckon so, George. Better listen up and hear what the Lord had to say to him."

George's eyes widened as he nodded somberly.

"Psalm 55:22 says, 'Cast thy burden upon the Lord, and he shall sustain thee: he shall never suffer the righteous to be moved.' I thought a great deal about this verse, folks, and felt confident that the Lord wanted me to see something important in it. You know when the silver played out here in Temperance, most of our rowdier folks took their leave. Temperance is now just a shadow of the boom town it once was but the atmosphere is purer and the lifestyle better. I know a lot of you are suffering and most of you don't know from day to day how much longer you'll be able to hold out, but I don't think the Lord will allow you to suffer or to be moved. We need to cast this problem upon Him and know that He is faithful to deliver us."

A few "Amens" resounded in the log-framed structure and Pastor Brokamp smiled. Before he could continue, however, a blast of winter air hit the congregation from the opened church door.

Zandy turned to see a tall, dark-haired man enter the building, close the doors behind him, and stroll boldly to the front of the church.

For the briefest of moments her hazel eyes met his brown-black ones. Before she quickly lowered her gaze, Zandy noticed the slightest smile form on his lips.

Everyone expected the stranger to take a seat but, when he kept walking until he reached the pulpit, most couldn't contain their surprise. A rustling murmur of comments moved through the church as the stranger spoke momentarily with Pastor Brokamp.

"If I may have everyone's attention," Pastor Brokamp said excitedly, "I believe the Lord is about to reveal Himself in a mighty way."

Zandy forgot the young boys who fidgeted beside her and felt drawn, almost captivated, by the man. She watched him as intently as did the rest of the congregation, but he seemed more than once to focus his attention in her direction. Why did she feel that he would forever change her destiny?

"Friends," the stranger began in a rich, baritone voice, "I am Riley Dawson."

So the face has a name, Zandy thought to herself, wondering at the same time what could have brought this well-dressed man of means to the tiny town of Temperance.

"I have recently purchased a great deal of the property in Temperance and have it on the best authority that silver will once again run rich from this town."

You could've heard a pin drop, Zandy thought to herself as the people stared in stunned silence. They feared to hope that the man was right and at the same time couldn't help but wonder what it possibly had to do with them.

"I wanted to come to you straight off and explain my plans and solicit your help," Riley continued before anyone could speak or move. "It is my desire to make Temperance, Colorado, a boom town again."

This created a stir and more than one person poised the unspoken question of "How?" in their eyes. While his attention seemed turned to the opposite side of the room, Zandy allowed herself the privilege of studying Riley Dawson. He, however, quickly returned his gaze to where she sat, causing Zandy to go crimson realizing that he knew she'd been considering him quite intently. His slight smile did nothing to ease her embarrassment, and even Burley turned to his daughter to find her most uncomfortable from the attention.

Riley would have laughed aloud had his plan not been so important. He was most captivated by the dark-headed woman who sat amidst four bored children. Surely they weren't hers, he thought as he waited for the rumbling excitement to die down. No, he reasoned to himself, most likely they were her brothers or perhaps a neighbor's children. This thought seemed to offer him yet another direction of consideration and wasn't at all helping him to concentrate on the task at hand.

"I would like," Riley began, "to hire as many of you who care to work. There will of course be mining jobs, but also there will be a need to place people in supportive jobs like running stores, cooking, laundering, schooling—all the things that a prosperous boom town would have."

A man in the front row who Zandy knew ran a small

general store, spoke up. "Who's going to grubstake the stores with the supplies they need for this boom? I ain't got the money to bring in freighters full of goods."

"Mister?" Riley questioned for a name.

"Edwards, Tim Edwards," the man said rather grudgingly.

"Mister Edwards, I plan to grubstake the business dealings in this town. Of course, it will be for an interest in the business," Riley added.

"Of course," Mr. Edwards replied sarcastically. "Nothing ever comes free. I guess you'll want most of the profits for such a thing."

"Not at all," Riley said in what sounded like disinterest. "I will expect to be paid a fair price for the goods but beyond this I only expect ten percent of your profits."

The crowd burst into excited chatter. Was this man being honest with them? Could this be the deliverance that they'd prayed for? The news even surprised Zandy who, although she was no business authority, had always had a good head for figures and an avid interest in business. Riley Dawson was offering the town a way back onto its feet and for a relatively inexpensive cost.

Riley continued to explain his plans for the "company" town as he called it, assuring everyone that there would be work for all and that everyone would share the wealth. After announcing that he would have another meeting the following evening, Riley stepped down from the pulpit and was immediately rushed by several members of the community.

Pastor Brokamp, seeing that the evening's meeting

was of little interest in light of Riley Dawson's announcement, offered a word of benediction and joined the gathering crowd to ask Riley questions.

Burley Stewart scratched his chin thoughtfully. "Sounds too good to be true," he muttered under his breath.

"It does sound good," Zandy offered while trying to free her long braided hair from George's playful hands. "Are you going to go talk to him?"

Her father hesitated a moment and, before he could answer, found that Riley Dawson had come to him.

"I'm Riley Dawson," he said as he extended his hand and Burley took it quickly in greeting.

"I'm Burley Stewart." Zandy heard her father answer. "This here is my oldest daughter, Alexandra, and my four boys."

"And your wife?" Riley questioned, all the while watching Zandy's lowered face.

"She's back at our place. Just gave birth to a new young'un last night," Burley said proudly.

"Congratulations, Mister Stewart."

"Ah, just call me Burley; everybody does."

"All right," Riley said with a smile.

George jumped from Zandy's lap and fairly flew across the pew to tell Riley all about his new sister. "She's got no hair," George said in his little boy voice, "and I think she's ugly."

Riley laughed heartily and Zandy reached out and pulled George back into her arms. George protested but Zandy knew how to manage him.

"I wouldn't worry too much about her looks right

now," Riley said as he stared with brazen intensity into Zandy's face. "Just look at her big sister. She's turned out pleasant enough. Just give her time."

Zandy blushed scarlet and felt her face grow as hot as if she had a fever. She buried her face against George as he arched in protest against her firm grip. What a bold thing to say about someone in front of their father, Zandy thought silently.

If the moment caused Riley anything more than the slightest thought, Zandy couldn't tell. The words continued to haunt her, however, long after she'd followed her father and brothers back to the cabin.

As she dressed for bed, Zandy continued to think about Riley Dawson. She pulled out of memory every detail of every word he'd spoken. She remembered how his eyes had stripped away all thought of pretense and left Zandy feeling emotionally bared to his penetrating scrutiny.

There was something very powerful in this man and something very dangerous, Zandy decided. She sat down and brushed her long brown hair, pulling the brush through over and over as she pondered the man behind the name of Riley Dawson.

two

"This is going to change everything," Burley Stewart told his wife as she nursed their new daughter. "Riley Dawson has promised jobs to anyone who wants one. I'm telling you, Ruth, our bad days are behind us. We'll soon be eating our white bread again, you'll see."

Ruth seemed unconvinced. At thirty-six, she felt worn out and tired. To even hope that Riley Dawson could deliver them from poverty was too much to expect. "Burley, we have six kids, though Zandy I'm sure will be marrying in a year or two, and they have to have food to eat and clothes to wear. We aren't getting any younger and we need to be realistic."

Zandy tried not to listen in on the conversation but in a small, three-room house, with nothing but tar paper walls and canvas to buffer the words, it wasn't difficult to overhear every word that was said.

Zandy understood how her stepmother felt. Back in Missouri the entire family had known relative security and comfort. Ruth in fact had left a very comfortable home in order to marry Burley Stewart. Ruth Stewart had once been Zandy's school teacher and, after the death of Zandy's mother, she'd quickly become a godsend to both Zandy and her father. Zandy loved Ruth with all her heart and daily thanked God for her. It wasn't often that a person was blessed not only with one loving mother, but two.

Burley continued to explain Riley's propositions while Ruth, ever the conservative when it came to risk, was trying to understand her husband's dream. Zandy found herself praying that Riley Dawson was everything he claimed to be and that the town of Temperance, Colorado, was indeed about to be delivered from poverty and certain death.

After going through her day's chores in a preoccupied manner, Zandy made her way with her father and the boys to the meeting at town hall.

The meeting hall was larger than the church, but not by much. The room was thirty feet across and another forty feet long but, with no more than thirty permanent residents, half of whom were children, the hall was plenty big enough to accommodate everyone.

Riley Dawson stood at the front of the room surrounded by six rough-looking men, all of who wore gun belts complete with revolvers.

Zandy steered the boys to seats at the back of the hall and watched as her father made his way toward the front. Zandy knew that he intended to sit close to the front in order to be a part of any discussion or decision, but Zandy was happy enough to stay toward the back of the room.

She'd barely taken her seat when she looked up to find Riley's eyes fixed unyieldingly upon her. So as not to offend him, she offered the briefest smile and then turned her attention to Bart who was trying to show her his latest scratch. Totally immersed in the young boy's conversation, Zandy didn't realize that Riley had come to stand beside her.

"Why not come sit up at the front?" Riley questioned.

The richness of his deep voice caused Zandy to tremble slightly. "I have to take care of my brothers," Zandy said as she nervously pulled George onto her lap. "It's really best for everyone else if we stay back here. You know, in case the boys get noisy."

Riley smiled, and Zandy couldn't help but notice the brilliant white, perfectly lined teeth. He wasn't what people would call a handsome man, he was in fact much too rugged looking for that, but he was attractive. Zandy tried not to make an open study of his appearance, but it was difficult to hide her curiosity.

"I yield to your wisdom, Miss Stewart," Riley said in a rather formal tone. "However, you would be doing me a great honor if you would allow me to call on you in the future."

Zandy was stunned. She knew that there were very few women in the town on which a gentleman could come calling, but of those available souls, Zandy also knew she wasn't the most attractive or promising.

"I suppose it would be best to talk to my father," Zandy replied softly. Then concern crept into her mind and washed her soul with doubt. Perhaps he hadn't meant to call on her in a romantic way.

Riley seemed to sense her misgivings and smiled again. "Of course, you are right. I must apologize for having forgotten my manners." Zandy let out a sigh of relief before Riley continued. "I must take my leave for the time, however. It seems to be necessary to get this meeting started."

Zandy nodded but said nothing more. Her throat felt strangely dry and even when Joshua pressed closer and asked her how much longer they'd have to sit there, Zandy found it impossible to answer.

The meeting itself was only slightly longer than the announcement at the church. Riley introduced the six rough-looking characters as the new law and order in the town. Zandy knew three of the men as former residents, in fact one man, Jim Williams, had even taken Zandy to a church social last fall. The other two, Tom and Jake Atkins, were brothers who always seemed to be in a row with someone and often with each other. Rounding out this number were Mike Muldair, K.C. Russell, and Pat Folkes.

Riley explained that these men would be his eyes and ears among the townspeople and that if anyone had a problem that needed Riley's attention, they could take it to one of his six hired men first. Although Temperance had never had much in the way of a law official, no one seemed to mind Riley's plan, nor the fact that he simply announced how things would be and didn't ask, even once, for anyone's opinion.

The rest of the meeting passed in mild chaos. Riley directed everyone to put themselves in the hands of his six men, who, in turn, showed the townspeople how to go about signing up for work.

While Zandy continued to contemplate Riley Dawson, George grew bored and fell asleep in her arms. Something about him seemed quite appealing and yet there was something else that seemed sinister and foreboding.

Two days later, mule-train freighters brought in several wagonloads of supplies. The general store's shelves were restocked to overflowing and two new hardware stores opened up.

The town's former seamstress teamed up with two other women to open a tailoring and laundry business, while at Riley's suggestion a bakery and restaurant were assigned to two different families.

Within three weeks the silver mines were showing color and word was out that Temperance was well on its way to becoming a boom town to equal Leadville and Central City.

Burley had taken a job in the mines and Riley, sensing his ability to lead, had put him in charge of the day shift. As men began to pour into the town looking for work at the mine as well as filing claims of their own, Burley was content to be able to provide his exorbitant earnings of five dollars a day to feed and clothe his family.

Others in town fared just as well. Those who'd been part of the original plan did better than those who came after news of the boom reached Denver and other places, but Riley was more than generous with everyone. In fact the generosity was so well received that when the regular weekly town meeting took place, the citizens of Temperance voted to change the name of their town to Dawson, and they elected Riley their new mayor.

In the meantime, Zandy was enjoying the fact that the spring thaw had begun. Every day Corner Creek would melt and the run off would make muddy rivers of the town's streets. Then at night it would freeze over again producing a light frosting of ice on the pathways throughout Dawson. Zandy had heard the old-timers say that it could go on like this for a month or more, but she didn't mind. It was the forerunner to the warmth and greenery that would be spring proper. That alone made any inconvenience worthwhile.

Zandy hummed through her work and, in spite of the fact that the tiny three-room house was drafty and dowdy, she did her best to add cheery touches here and there.

When they'd first arrived, despite the fact that both Zandy and Ruth seriously doubted the stability of the shoddily placed house frame, they had nailed several small crates, bottom sides to the wall, and had made cupboards and shelves in which to put their meager supplies. Then Ruth, having read in one of her ladies' magazines about the fashionable elegance of tasseled drapings, took a small piece of calico and clipped a tassel from a once-stylish dancing slipper, then sewed these together to form her own touch of refinement. This was then placed just as the magazine suggested across the top of the old crate, with the tassel hanging ever so conspicuously over the side. Both Ruth and Zandy had thought themselves to be quite stylish with this new addition.

Zandy smiled at this memory as she picked up a seed catalog and sat down at the kitchen table. It was only a matter of minutes before Ruth walked into the kitchen and joined Zandy at the table.

"I see you're looking through the catalog. Just what did you have in mind, Zandy?" Ruth questioned and tried her best to suppress a cough. She was pale and sickly, still not having quite recovered from childbirth. This greatly worried Zandy, but she said nothing that gave away her concern.

"Well," Zandy began, "aside from the vegetables we planned, I thought about planting some herbs and maybe even a rose bush or two. Does that sound terribly frivolous, Ruth?"

Ruth smoothed out the flour sack tablecloth and smiled. "Not at all. I remember how beautiful the roses were back at our house in Missouri. Could it have been only last summer when we said goodbye to them?"

Zandy reached out her hand to cover her stepmother's. She felt the same twinge of pain at the memory of home that Ruth did. Temperance, or Dawson as it was now called, had never felt like home, and Zandy doubted seriously that it ever would.

Ruth began to cough again, and Zandy couldn't help but frown. "You need to see a doctor, Ruth," Zandy said with great concern in her voice. "That cough is getting worse, and Molly needs you to be healthy. I heard Riley say that a company doctor would be arriving within the week. I'm going to check into it and see that he comes here first thing."

"We can't afford to be extravagant, Zandy. We've only managed to put aside a few dollars. I can't expect Burley to waste his hard-earned pay on a doctor. I'll be fine."

"Getting a doctor for you is not extravagant. I've already put the boys to work reading and printing their letters in the back room. I'll be just a few minutes and hopefully when I return, I'll bring the town's doctor with me."

Zandy got to her feet and untied her apron. Ruth really did look quite ill, and a grave thought crossed Zandy's mind. What if Ruth died? This country was hard on everyone, and the weaker the individual the more the elements took their toll. Ruth was a city girl and while she'd been able to bear four children with little trouble, this time was different. Fear of the grippe or consumption ran rampant during the winter months, especially in the poorer conditions of towns like Dawson.

Molly began to cry from the bedroom, so Zandy helped Ruth to her feet. "You try to rest as much as possible after you feed her," Zandy said as though she had reversed roles with her stepmother.

"I will, Zandy. I promise," Ruth said, hoping that the raised eyebrows and furrowed forehead of her stepdaughter would calm.

Zandy pulled on her coat and made the muddy journey into town.

Dawson was really no different than any other mountain mining town. It was dirty and had all the characteristics of having been slapped together overnight, which of course it had been.

The life of a mining town was often short lived and thus most of the buildings in town were nothing more than tents. Once a town proved it's color in showing a solid vein of ore, then building materials would be freighted in to make more substantial buildings.

When the town had been called Temperance, it had

known a wealthy time, and so in its favor now stood several wood-and-brick buildings, clapboard houses, and even a stately mansion that seemed to rise up out of the ground at the north end of the town. Zandy glanced in the direction of the mansion knowing full well that it was now the residence of Riley Dawson.

"Miss Zandy!"

Zandy glanced up to see Jim Williams walking toward her.

"Hello, Jim," Zandy said with a smile. "It feels like the temperature has warmed up quite a bit."

"I'll say. Corner Creek is flooding again," the dark-haired Jim said, knowing that it wasn't any real news.

"Yes, I've seen the mess. It's a good thing you told me what to expect. If you hadn't, I would have worried that we were about to slide on down the mountain with the mud." Zandy allowed Jim to walk alongside her while she continued to make her way toward the board-walk. "Jim, have you any news of the doctor?" Zandy questioned, suddenly remembering Jim's connection to Riley's administration of Dawson.

"He arrived just this morning. He's up at the Travis mansion," Jim said and paused, "I guess I mean Dawson mansion."

"Yes, I heard that Mister Dawson had taken up residence there. I'm sure he was the only one who could afford the price. Do you know if the doctor will be staying there? I mean, I heard that some of the new lawmen were staying in the cottage behind the big house."

"Riley's been real generous," Jim said as he helped

Zandy to step up on the boardwalk. She allowed his touch only for a moment before making the pretense of smoothing out her long linsey-woolsey skirt. Jim took the hint and dropped his hand before expanding on Riley Dawson's many virtues. "Riley Dawson must have had quite a grubstake. You know he won the deeds to the first five mine claims."

"Won? You mean he gambled for the mines?" Zandy questioned, finding herself far more interested in Riley Dawson than she wanted to be.

"That's right. I hear he's quite a card player. I figure it's how he got enough money together to buy all of that new fancy mining equipment. Not to mention all of the money he's been shelling out for salaries and store goods," Jim replied with a look around him to make certain no one would overhear him. "He's paying me four dollars a day. Imagine that! Four dollars a day, and I don't even have to go down into the mines and breathe the dust. I wasn't even making four dollars a day when I was double jacking with your pa," Jim said, hoping that Zandy would think more favorably toward him after remembering the closeness he'd shared with her father.

Zandy cringed at the thought of the dangerous job. Double jacking was usually done by two, and sometimes three, men. One man would hold the long steel drill bit while the other man would pound the bit with an eight-pound hammer, alternating with a third man if available. All this was done in order to make blasting holes in the face rock of the mine. Once this was done, the holes were packed with "giant," a lethal and unstable explosive known to most as dynamite.

"I remember," Zandy said as she issued a silent prayer that her father would tire of this dangerous life and take them all back to Missouri.

Without sensing Zandy's disillusionment, Jim continued. "There aren't going to be any double jackers in Riley's mines. He's bringing in Burleigh drills."

"What are they?" Zandy asked, wondering if they would bring her father help or harm.

"Steam-operated drills. They're something to behold. I saw one up in Georgetown. They cut down the time it takes to drill the blasting holes and decrease the risk of losing fingers or busting a guy's hand while jacking."

"Sounds good, but are they safe?" Zandy asked as she stopped in front of the general store.

"Safe as anything ever is in a mine," Jim offered with a look that told it all. "I'm just glad to be doing what I'm doing." Zandy nodded and started to go into the store. "Say, weren't you wanting the doctor?"

"Yes," Zandy said as if suddenly remembering why she'd come to town in the first place. "Could you send him to our place? Ruth isn't well."

"I sure will. Hope it's nothing serious," Jim said and smiled. "I was kind of hoping that you'd be coming to the dance Saturday night."

"I'd really like to Jim, but if Ruth is still doing poorly she'll need me at home," Zandy said and silently prayed that Ruth would be well enough.

"Can I check with you on Friday?" Jim asked hopefully.

"I'd like that, Jim," Zandy said, matching the smile on his face with one of her own.

three

The knock at the door startled Zandy. The rest of the family, including a much-restored Ruth, had already departed for the Saturday night festivities, and she wasn't expecting anyone. Opening the door, Zandy took a step back, surprised to find Riley Dawson standing in the doorway.

"I'm sorry if I frightened you," Riley began. "I happened to notice that your family had already left for the dance and wondered if you would be joining them."

Zandy noted Riley's refined appearance and the stylish cut of his expensive suit. There wouldn't be another in Dawson dressed as well as this man. "I was just frosting a cake," Zandy finally spoke. "I promised to bring it for the refreshment table."

"I see," Riley said as he appraised Zandy's gown. The bright red basque and the red plaid sateen of the bustled skirt were as lovely as any that Riley had seen in Denver.

Zandy noted the look of appreciation in Riley's eyes and laughed to herself. Perhaps Riley wouldn't find her so smartly dressed if he knew that she'd had to make her own bustle by tying a string through an old tin can. The silence made an awkward barrier between them and Zandy found herself wishing that Riley would leave. Instead, Riley asked if he could wait for her and accom-

26

pany her to the dance.

Zandy frowned slightly, remembering that Jim intended to meet her at the dance. "I'm not sure that would be appropriate," Zandy said reluctantly.

"And what could possibly be inappropriate about it?" Riley said with a grin. The smile quickly turned into a frown however, as he stepped into the house. "How can you live like this?" he questioned without waiting for an answer to his first question.

Zandy was taken aback by Riley's open criticism. "I beg your pardon?" The cake was totally forgotten as Zandy followed Riley as he boldly made his way through the small house.

"This is deplorable. How many people are living here?"

"Eight, and I'd like to ask you what right do you have to trespass?" Zandy questioned rather indignantly. "I don't recall having invited you to take a tour of our accommodations, and so I would like you to leave."

Riley turned from the poverty before him and stared boldly into Zandy's fiery green eyes. His eyes narrowed slightly as he considered the woman before him. He liked the spunk that Zandy displayed in the fearless defense of her home.

"I didn't mean to offend you," Riley began, "it's just that I can't believe the conditions here. It's not that you haven't done wonders with it," he said as he waved his hand, "but to be honest, Miss Stewart, I can't imagine that this is a healthy place in which adults, much less children, can live."

Zandy dropped her guard. She had to admit that Riley

was right, and the sorrow showed clearly on her face.

"I'm sorry," Riley said softly. "I know it must be hard to live like this."

"I do worry about the children," Zandy said as she walked back to the kitchen. She picked up the bowl of frosting and, after stirring it briefly, poured the contents on the top of her cake and smoothed it out with a knife.

"I could help," Riley said in an ominous way that made Zandy regret having been honest.

"I don't think we should discuss it any further," Zandy stated firmly as she finished with the cake.

"There's no need to feel uncomfortable, Miss Stewart. I own this property."

Zandy's eyes opened wide in surprise. "You?"

Riley crossed his arms. "Why should that surprise you? I own most of Dawson."

"I just presumed that my father owned this place. We owned our house back in Missouri," Zandy's little girl voice appealed to Riley in a way that he couldn't explain.

"I'm sorry to disillusion you. This house is on part of the claim that I took control of."

"You mean that you won, don't you? I heard that you gambled for the claims you now own."

Riley shrugged his shoulders. "So what if I did. These are hard and lawless times, Miss Stewart. Men come here with gold and silver fever so fierce that they stake everything they have. They don't care what it costs them to buy the equipment they need, and they don't care what they have to do to get a claim."

"Are there truly so many godless people?" Zandy

whispered more to herself than for any answer Riley might offer.

"Godless and worse," Riley admitted.

"What could possibly be worse than living without God?" Zandy questioned, suddenly fearful that Riley was one of those among the godless.

"Believe me," Riley cocked his head ever so slightly and with an intense darkening to his dark eyes continued, "you don't want to know. There are men out there who would not only sell their own souls, but the soul of anyone else that stood in their way."

Zandy felt a chill go down her spine. She knew she'd led a sheltered life, but never had she really stopped to imagine that such sufferings and dealings were really going on in the world.

Only the table stood between Zandy and Riley and the rich aroma of the butter frosting was quickly overwhelmed by the expensive cologne that Riley Dawson wore. Zandy was fast realizing just how out of place she felt with Riley.

"I'm sorry again if I've frightened you," Riley said, thinking that Zandy looked much like a person who'd seen a ghost. "A young woman like yourself can't be too careful these days. But again, I could do much to help you."

Zandy nervously dropped the knife, and it made a clattering sound on the table before falling silently to the dirt floor below.

Riley reached out and took hold of Zandy's hand. He could feel her tremble beneath his touch, and the response excited him. "Come sit with me," Riley said in such a way that Zandy could only follow him as he led her to the makeshift sofa at the opposite side of the room.

"Miss Stewart," Riley said as he motioned for Zandy to sit, "may I call you Alexandra?"

Zandy nodded silently and then added, "Most folks call me Zandy."

Riley smiled, once again revealing perfect teeth. "I shall call you by both. Alexandra for more serious moments, and Zandy for less formal occasions."

"And which is this?" Zandy found herself whispering.

"This is quite serious," Riley said as he came to sit beside Zandy.

"I see," Zandy said as she tried to put a bit more space between herself and the tycoon. There was something very dangerous about this man, and yet Zandy didn't really comprehend what it was that made her so cautious in dealing with Riley Dawson.

"Alexandra, you can change everything for your family and for yourself. I can provide a new home, plenty of food for the children, and coal for the stove."

"And just what is it that I have to do?" Alexandra asked suspiciously.

"It's nothing all that difficult. I want a companion, someone I can lavish with gifts and attention. Someone who will act as hostess in my house for the many parties I intend to have. And someone who will be there after the parties are over. Do you understand me, Alexandra?" Riley asked in a low whisper that made Zandy feel very uncomfortable.

"But you barely know me, Mister Dawson," Zandy

began. "I can't imagine asking me to take such an important position in your life without having even the slightest knowledge of who I am and what my past is."

"I know enough. I know that you're pure and innocent. You've never been married, although that does amaze me. You're loving and giving; always quick to lend a hand to your father and stepmother; and you care well for your brothers and sister. Beyond that I know that you're by far the most beautiful woman I've ever met."

"Now I know you've gone mad," Zandy laughed. "There are many more beautiful women in this world, not to mention this town. I'm not at all the refined and fashionable woman that would do justice to your image."

"The material parts I can create. Refinement and fashion are often nothing more than the clothes on your back and the shoes on your feet. Think about it. Don't you feel quite smart in your party dress? Don't you in fact walk differently when you put slippers on your feet in place of brogans?"

Zandy thought of the heavy brogans she usually wore to fight through the muddy streets of Dawson. The unflattering boot shoes were nearly impossible to tell right from left, and they weighed at least a pound a piece. She had to admit that Riley was right about the shoes. The look on her face told him everything.

"See, I was right, wasn't I?" Riley said and without waiting for an answer, continued. "I can buy you the finest clothes that were ever created for a woman to wear. Rich sateens and velvets, opulent silks, and fine ermine for trims. I can put jewels around your neck to rival the Queen of England's. But, more than this, I can put balanced meals in the stomachs of your brothers and sister. I can give them proper clothing and a house with real walls and bedrooms."

Zandy shifted uncomfortably. This was her first real proposal and she was quite taken aback by the dashing man who promised her everything that a woman could ever want.

"But what of love?" Zandy found herself speaking without thought.

"That's a rather bold question for a young girl," Riley replied with a quizzically raised eyebrow. "What makes you think that I wouldn't consider such a thing just as important as you do? The chemistry must be right between a man and a woman in order to spend their days and nights together." Zandy blushed crimson at the words. "Just remember," Riley continued, "you are the one that brought up the subject."

"I didn't expect you to get vulgar," Zandy said stiffly. She tried to get to her feet but Riley took hold of her arm and pulled her back.

"I believe, given the importance of this situation, you would do well to stay and hear me out," Riley said in a rather brusque manner.

The tone of his voice left Zandy cold, and she turned to find his hand still gripping her arm rather tightly. "You're hurting me, Mister Dawson," Zandy said with exacting control given to each word. In truth she felt like crying or at best running, but Burley Stewart had not raised his daughter to be a coward. "Take your hand off of me if you expect me to continue considering your proposal. I can't agree to marry a man who would treat his wife so rudely."

Riley laughed out loud and not only removed his hand but jumped to his feet. The action so surprised Zandy that she could only stare open mouthed.

"I'm not looking for a wife, Alexandra," Riley said, composing himself once again.

"You're not looking for a wife? Then what is this all about?" Zandy questioned.

"Alexandra, you are so very naive and innocent. I find that very attractive. It's one of the biggest reasons I chose you," Riley stated as calmly as if he were discussing production at the mine.

"Chose me for what?"

"I want you to be my mistress, Alexandra."

"You what?" Zandy questioned as she got to her feet. "I can't believe you came here to insult me in such a manner. Of all the nerve! Get out of my house!" Zandy was nearly hysterical as she rushed to the door and opened it to the cold April night air.

"It isn't that simple," Riley said firmly as he refused to move. "I am used to getting what I want, and I want you."

"I don't care what you want. You may own most of this town, but you certainly don't own me. You can't force me to live with you."

"And just why can't I?" Riley asked in such a matter-of-fact way that Zandy began to fear that perhaps he could.

"Kidnapping is against the law," Zandy whispered.

A smiled played at the corners of Riley's lips. "You forget, I am the law here. Besides, it wouldn't be kidnapping."

"Taking someone against their will is kidnapping and anyway, you aren't the only law. I believe in a higher form of law—God's law. I am a Christian as is my father and stepmother, and they'd never allow such a hideous thing to take place."

"Alexandra, you don't seem to understand just how miserable I can make life for you and your precious family."

Riley's words chilled Zandy through and through. Slowly, she closed the door, detesting the look of satisfaction on Riley's face.

"My family has certainly done nothing to merit your wrath, Mister Dawson."

"Call me Riley."

"Riley," Zandy said, hoping that by yielding this small request Riley would be content to drop the matter. "My family is not the issue here, and I don't believe you're being fair by including them."

"Fairness has little to do with this issue nor with life. I have found very little to be fair. Consider for yourself the difficult job your father has in the mines. He works long shifts in dank and dangerous circumstances for a mere pittance of what the job's worth. On the other hand, I have amassed a fortune by sitting down in refined clothes, eating the best food, and drinking the best the house has to offer, all while turning over a few cards. There is nothing fair about it but, nonetheless, that's life."

"It's not our life," Zandy said with a sudden renewal of strength. "God doesn't intend for us to live our lives at the expense of others. We are to treat others better than ourselves and to be kind to our enemies." She emphasized the word "enemies" hoping that Riley would take it as a personal reference.

"I would remind you, Alexandra," Riley's voice was now a deadly sword poised at Zandy's heart. "I can put an end to your family. Children don't survive long without food and shelter. Your father hasn't put aside enough money to get his family out of Dawson and, though your stepmother is feeling better, without medication the consumption will no doubt kill her."

"Consumption? The doctor said nothing about consumption," Zandy said as her hand flew to her throat. The growing ache there was threatening to choke her.

"Your stepmother is a very sick woman. My doctor has medicine that will help her, but I can easily deny the help and your stepmother will die."

"What a cruel and vicious man you are! Why, I wouldn't even want to court you much less live in an unholy manner with you. How can you live with yourself?" Zandy backed against the door as Riley stepped toward her.

"It's true that I can be rather cruel, but I can also be very generous and loving. You must turn the tables in this situation, however, and realize that it isn't me, but you who will deny your family these things." Riley opened the door and stepped into the darkness. "It's a great deal to consider, is it not?"

Zandy looked at him in total confusion. "Me? How

can you possibly say this cruelty would be my fault? You are asking me to go against the law of my God and Savior. You want me to deny the principles of God's Word for the desires of a lustful man? And somehow, in my denial of such an immoral path, you tell me my family's fate is in my hands."

Riley sunk his hands deep into his pockets and smiled. "Life is full of compromises and concessions, Alexandra. There are worse fates in life than to be my mistress. In fact, I think you would find the kind of life I could give you would far outweigh the spiritual misgivings that you might have."

"How very irreverent you are toward God, Mister Dawson! God is my rock and my deliverance from evil. I don't fear you or anything you can do." With that Zandy slammed the door in Riley's face and threw herself into the nearest chair to pray.

"Dear God, what manner of evil is this man? Please protect us from Riley Dawson and keep me safe from his advances."

Suddenly, the words of 1 John 2:16 and 17 came to Zandy from somewhere in her memory. "For all that is in the world, the lust of the flesh, and the lust of the eyes, and the pride of life, is not of the Father, but is of the world. And the world passeth away, and the lust thereof: but he that doeth the will of God abideth for ever."

It was quite clear that Riley Dawson was not of the Father, Zandy thought and she shuddered to think of the future that he intended for her.

four

The cold of winter eventually melted into the delicate warmth of spring days. With it came the anticipated gardens and outdoor activities that everyone had missed during the seemingly endless winter.

Zandy tried to keep her mind on the rows of newly planted vegetables, but her memories kept taking her back to Riley Dawson and the fact that he expected her to become his mistress.

She'd wanted so much to talk to someone about the situation, but, with Ruth's illness, Zandy refused to make more of a burden for her stepmother, and her father was always working or sleeping. Besides, Zandy reasoned, he would be quite angry with Riley for such a suggestion and it could very well cost her father his job.

Before picking up her hoe and returning to the house, Zandy gave the last plant a brief pat of dirt around its base. Next, there were shopping chores to complete, and Zandy hated these more than anything for the way they forced her to come under the scrutiny of the townspeople, in particular, Riley's hired men. She'd learned rather quickly that Riley was having her watched, for there were far too many times she looked over her shoulder to find one of the six so-called lawmen, watching and waiting for her next move.

Then, Zandy remembered, there were the inevitable times when she was alone and Riley would just happen to appear from out of nowhere to badger and hound her about his request.

Zandy looked in briefly on Ruth and Molly. Both were sleeping soundly, and Zandy had to admit that the medicine the doctor prescribed had made quite a difference in her stepmother's health. The boys were at the neighbor's house, and so Zandy made a list of the things she needed, found her market basket, and braved the short walk into town.

When Zandy reached the end of the narrow lane, she was almost stunned at the way Dawson had grown almost overnight. Tents had been erected everywhere, and the main street of downtown was flooded with people. Dawson now sported seven saloons and four eating establishments, as well as a new bank building and a bevy of shops that Zandy would have never expected to see in the small town.

As if on cue, Jim Williams exited the jailhouse with K.C. and Pat at his side. Before Jim crossed the street to join Zandy, he said something to the two men that took them off down the street in a hurry.

"Hello, Jim," Zandy said apprehensively as Jim approached.

"Hello," Jim said as he touched his finger to his hat. "I haven't seen you in a while. Have you been sick?"

Zandy grimaced and said, "No, I just don't like having Riley Dawson keeping tabs on me."

Jim tried hard not to look surprised, but Zandy could

tell he wasn't at all happy that she'd brought up the subject. "Sorry, Zandy. I don't like this game, either."

"Then why do you play it?" Zandy asked rather brusquely.

"Look, Zandy, I have to work and I don't have enough to leave Dawson. Not yet anyway," Jim offered.

"I'm sorry, Jim. It's just that I don't like people keeping track of me. I suppose Riley will be here shortly so I'd best get my shopping done before he ruins my whole day," Zandy said and went into the general store.

Jim followed her inside, still trying to explain his position. "You know how much I like you, Zandy. I can't stand the fact that Dawson has his eye on you, but there's not much I can do about it. I don't have enough money for us to get married and besides, if we got married, Riley would fire me just as quickly."

Zandy whirled on her heel. "Married? We've never even talked of such things. You're being mighty bold today, Jim Williams." Zandy knew that he didn't deserve the anger that she was pouring out upon him but, after weeks of Riley Dawson's games, Zandy was rather tense.

Jim lowered his head, reminding Zandy of George when he was in trouble. "I just thought maybe if you knew how serious I was you could tell Riley that you weren't interested in him."

Zandy moved the basket she'd brought with her from one arm to the other, before taking hold of Jim's arm and pulling him with her to an unoccupied spot in the store. "I told Riley Dawson that I wasn't interested, Jim. I told him I detested him and wanted him to leave me alone.

I have never met a more deplorable man in my life. But," Zandy sighed, "he doesn't care. I can't tell you everything, but Riley Dawson is a dangerous man, and I don't intend to get tangled up with the likes of him."

When the bell on the door rang, Zandy knew without looking up that Riley would be the one to enter the store. That's the way it always went whenever Zandy came to town. How she wished that Ruth would get well and feel like making the trip. Zandy had even sent Joshua once before only to have the store owner refuse to allow the boy to access the Stewart credit line.

"You'd best check in with your boss," Zandy said as she left Jim and started to pick up the items on her list.

By making sideways glances, Zandy could see that Jim was talking with Riley at the front door. She moved quickly around the store picking up sugar, thread, and a package of needles.

"Can I help you, Miss Stewart?" Zandy glanced up to find Mister Edwards, the store's owner.

"Yes," Zandy said as she studied her list. "I need three yards of white flannel."

"More diapers for Molly?" Mister Edwards questioned good naturedly while he went to the task of cutting the material.

"No," Zandy smiled. "Flour sacks will work well enough for that. I plan to make this into nightgowns for her. She's growing so fast, I'm having trouble keeping up with her."

"I can well imagine. Say, we've got cotton stockings at three pairs for a quarter," the man replied as he handed Zandy the material.

"Not today," Zandy said as she checked the list. "I do need some canned milk, though."

"Sure thing. How many?" he questioned as he reached behind the counter for the milk.

"Better give me six cans," Zandy said as she tried to make mental calculations on the total. She tried not to look toward the door, but she wanted most desperately to know whether Riley and Jim were still talking.

Riley stood alone leaning against the door frame, and he smiled broadly when Zandy looked his way. She immediately regretted the contact as her heart started to pound harder.

Placing the basket on the counter, Zandy waited while Mr. Edwards totaled her goods. He pulled out a black account book from the shelf behind the counter.

"Let's see, that's one dollar and thirty-five cents."

"Do we have enough balance on account?" Zandy questioned, hoping that she wouldn't have to part with the few precious coins she'd brought with her.

Mister Edwards looked up to check out Riley's response and, when he nodded, the older man wrote down the amount in his ledger. "You have more than enough here, Miss Stewart."

What a farce, Zandy thought to herself. How much longer was Riley Dawson going to insist on this madness?

Edwards placed all of Zandy's purchases in the basket and, with a smile, handed it back to her. "You come back soon."

Zandy nodded, took the basket, and buffeted herself against having to face Riley.

It had become a routine between them that Zandy would approach the door, and Riley would give her a wide sweeping bow before holding the door open for her to pass. Zandy said nothing as the moments played themselves out, and it wasn't until they were outside that Riley spoke to her.

"I've missed seeing you." His voice was warm and inviting, but Zandy knew it to be a dangerous trap.

"Sorry," she murmured and started to cross the street for home.

"Oh no, you don't," Riley said as he took hold of her arm and freed her hand from the weight of the basket. "I don't intend to let you get away that easily. You're having lunch with me."

"I'll do nothing of the kind," Zandy said, jerking her arm away from Riley's hold.

Riley's eyes narrowed slightly before he resecured his hold on Zandy's arm. "Don't make a scene. I just want to talk to you. Now, come along like a good girl and allow me to buy you lunch."

"No respectable woman would share refreshment with you," Zandy said, trying desperately to remain calm. "Besides, they're expecting me back at home."

"Then I'll walk you home and announce that you are coming to lunch with me."

"No!" Zandy exclaimed a bit more excitedly than she'd intended. "I'll come with you now."

"That's better," Riley said in the same self-satisfied tone he always took on when he got his way.

Zandy allowed Riley to help her cross the street and even managed to keep from saying anything when Riley continued to hold onto her long after it was necessary. She drew the line, however, when Riley suggested they dine in the lobby restaurant of the Neville Hotel, Dawson's newest sleeping establishment.

"I will not go into that place with you," Zandy said in a hushed whisper. Her voice was so low that Riley had to bend over to hear her repeat the words.

"And just why not? They have excellent food," Riley stated firmly.

"I'm not about to be seen going into a hotel with you. The Bible says that we should avoid even the appearance of evil. I'll not have people saying that I participated in something of this kind. If you insist on taking me to lunch, then take me somewhere that won't shame me."

Riley looked thunderstruck for a moment and just as quickly covered his surprise with determination. "It's either the Neville or my home. You make the choice."

Zandy looked into his eyes hoping to see some glimmer of hope that she might persuade him to change his mind. There was nothing there, however, except the danger she'd noted on the first night they'd met.

"What's it going to be, Alexandra?"

"Why do you insist on this pursuit, Riley?" Zandy asked boldly. "You know I'm not interested in your proposal. You know how I feel about the lifestyle you lead, so why continue with this game?"

Riley smiled and even the look in his eyes seemed to change. "It's not a game, my dear. It happens to be most important to me."

"You could have your pick of the saloon girls and

most any other respectable woman in town. Why continue to torment me? Look around you, Riley. There are more beautiful women in Dawson than ever before. Why not reconsider your choice? I promise not to be offended."

At this, Riley laughed and released his grip on Zandy's arm. With this bit of freedom, Zandy snatched the basket from Riley's hand and headed quickly down the boardwalk.

Undaunted by the fact that she knew Riley would angrily dog her heels, Zandy rushed headlong into the busy intersection, narrowly escaping an oncoming freighter only because Riley lifted her out of the way.

"Let me go!" Zandy exclaimed as Riley swung her around.

"I'm being heroic and saving your life. Have you no appreciation?" Riley said with a smile, but Zandy thought she read concern, almost fear, in his eyes.

"I'd rather you lent your heroic deeds to saving my virtue," Zandy replied.

Riley could see that his hands were full and that his demands had been met head-on. "You are the most stubborn woman I've ever met."

"Good," Zandy said and tossed her long braided hair over her shoulder. "I get the feeling it's about time someone stood up to you."

"People pay a price when they do," Riley said ominously.

Zandy began to make her way up the narrow mountain lane, not wanting to know what the price for her tenacity might be. Riley, however, had no intention of letting her challenge go unanswered and followed her.

"You see, Alexandra," Riley began, "I am a force to be reckoned with."

"So is a rattlesnake," Zandy said, braving a glance, but Riley didn't appear all that angry even in light of her frank protest.

"That's true and, like a rattlesnake, my bite can be most deadly."

"Meaning?" Zandy questioned as she stopped.

"Meaning, you can't ignore me and hope that I won't strike. I want you for my mistress, Alexandra. I won't change my mind and I won't choose another," Riley said matter-of-factly.

Zandy indignantly placed her market basket on the ground and, with arms akimbo, made her stand. "Why don't you just force yourself upon me, Mister Dawson? I mean, you find any and all opportunity to plague me with your presence. You have me watched so that you know when I'm alone and you hound my every step. I'm obviously not much to fight, and I certainly am no match for your strength. So, like the many other godless men you spoke of before, why not just take what you want and leave me alone!"

Zandy wasn't sure what kind of a reaction she expected but whatever it was, it certainly wasn't the laughter that came from Riley at that moment.

"You look positively grand, standing there with that wild look in your eye and the wind blowing across your face. You're flushed and out of breath and everything about you is radiant. I can't imagine even looking at another woman when you are nearby," Riley said in a way that made Zandy wish he would remain silent. "No, Alexandra, I won't force anything. Women come quite willingly to me. I can wait until you have a willing heart."

"It will never happen!" Zandy exclaimed as she reclaimed her basket and turned to leave.

Riley stopped her with a hand on her shoulder. "Remember my warning. I can make life most difficult for you and your family. I'm not asking for that much, Alexandra. Not really."

Zandy turned to face him. "Not asking for that much? I think you're either daft or completely incapable of reason. I will give myself willingly to the man of my choice, and he will be my husband in the eyes of God."

"Very well then, as they said when the silver first showed color, the rush is on," Riley said with a slight bow. "I hope you can live with the choice you've made."

five

Riley's retaliation came first in the form of shortened work hours for Burley. Instead of the regular eight-hour shift that Burley was used to, Zandy's father was stripped of his supervising duties and cut to six-hour days. In turn, Burley's paycheck was reduced as well.

Zandy saw the concern in her stepmother's eyes, but said nothing that might add to their grief. Burley tried to take it all in stride telling his family that God would look out for them as He always had but, in her heart, Zandy felt responsible.

The first few weeks weren't a problem. Ruth had managed to put aside a nice nest egg, and so they drew on it as they needed and tightened their belts as best they could.

Toward the end of June, however, the nest egg was depleted, and Burley's hours had been cut to half days. When Burley approached K.C. Russell about the matter, K.C. just shrugged his shoulders and told Burley he'd take it up with Riley and get back to him. Of course he never did and, while Burley was totally confused, Zandy knew only too well the reason.

The next blow came when they approached the store in order to buy groceries on credit. One by one the stores closed their doors to the Stewart family, and no amount of pleading would reopen them.

Zandy was more than just a little troubled by the turn of events, and she still couldn't bring herself to explain to her father that Riley Dawson was purposefully trying to force her into a compromising situation. It wasn't that she hadn't wanted to talk to her father. She had even tried once or twice to talk to him when he was alone, but she could never seem to find the right words. In the back of her mind Zandy blamed herself for the suffering and continuously wondered how she could right the wrong.

She sat in silence as her father put the last of the coal in the stove. "It'd be wise to take the young'uns to look for wood today, Zandy."

"Sure, Pa," Zandy replied as she looked up from the meager ration of oatmeal.

"I'm still hungry," Joshua whined as he cleaned out the last bits of oatmeal from his bowl.

"Here, have mine," Zandy said as she pushed her bowl over. "I'm not very hungry."

Ruth looked on in desperate consternation. She was trying to rock Molly and keep her mind from the misery that stared her in the face each day. How she wished they could leave and return to Missouri, but her love for Burley kept her silent.

Zandy was cleaning up the breakfast dishes when Ruth's gentle hand fell upon her shoulder. "You can't go on giving your food to the kids. You'll get sick."

"They need it worse than I do," Zandy said, refusing to look Ruth in the eye.

"What is it, Zandy? You haven't seemed yourself for weeks. Is there something I can help you with?"

"No, not really," Zandy said as she put away the

dishes.

Ruth sighed and took a seat at the table. "I know you're probably just as worried as I am. I honestly don't know what we're going to do. The kids never have enough to eat and, unless they beg something off the neighbors, they seem to suffer so."

"The garden should provide more," Zandy said as she joined her stepmother at the table, "especially since the weather has warmed up."

"But what do we do after that? What about this winter? If we only knew why Mister Dawson has cut your father's wages. Burley has tried three times to see Mister Dawson at his home, but those hired thugs of his just keep turning him away."

"I'm sure something will work out soon. I've been praying, and I know God won't let us down." Zandy hoped that she sounded convincing.

"I know He won't, Zandy," Ruth said with a smile. "God has never turned His back on us. I don't expect that He'll start now. Look, I have a little bit of change. I want you to go to Tim Edwards and explain that the kids have to have something to eat. Get whatever you can in the way of cornmeal and canned milk. I know it won't be much, but it'll be filling."

Zandy nodded and took the coins. "If Mister Edwards will even allow me in the store."

"He can't turn cash away," Ruth offered, and Zandy prayed that she was right.

After putting the boys to work collecting firewood, Zandy made her way into town. She remembered the verses that her father had read for their morning devotions. Psalm 141, verses eight and nine stuck in her memory. "But mine eyes are unto thee, O God the Lord: in thee is my trust; leave not my soul destitute. Keep me from the snares which they have laid for me. . . ."

"Yes, Lord," Zandy breathed, "keep me from the snares that Riley Dawson has laid for me."

The bell jingled as Zandy opened the door to Tim Edwards' general store. Zandy felt a bit of relief to see that no one else was inside the store, with the exception of Mister Edwards who was looking quite uncomfortable.

"Good morning, Mister Edwards," Zandy said as sweetly as she could muster. "I need cornmeal and canned milk."

"Miss Alexandra, I. . .uh. . .," the man looked completely at a loss for words.

"Here's the money. Just give me whatever you can," Zandy said, undaunted by his discomfort.

"I'm not supposed to trade with you," Edwards finally blurted out.

"Why not?" Zandy questioned.

Just then Riley Dawson stepped out from the back room. "I think we both know the answer to that question."

Zandy whirled around ready to do battle for her brothers and sister. "I have no idea what you mean, Mister Dawson. Has my family somehow offended you?"

Riley frowned as he studied Zandy for a moment. She was thinner, of this he was certain. Just the way her clothes were beginning to hang on her was evidence of this. No doubt she was giving away her share of food.

"No, Miss Stewart," Riley finally answered. "I'm simply being prudent."

"I have the cash, Mister Dawson. Now, may I have the goods or not?" Zandy refused to back down.

"Give her the food," Riley said, never taking his eyes from Zandy for even a moment.

Tim Edwards nodded, and Zandy could clearly read the relief in his eyes. He took her money and handed over the cornmeal and milk. Zandy turned on her heel, determined to ignore Riley's intense scrutiny but, as she moved toward the door, she could feel his eyes burning into her back.

"Allow me," Riley said as he was at her side in a moment. "I'll carry those things for you. Just to show you there's no hard feelings."

Zandy glared at him but allowed him to take the basket of goods from her hands. She wasn't about to give him the satisfaction of a scene.

Outside, Riley took hold of her elbow and helped her down from the boardwalk and across the street. Zandy remained silent, determined to say nothing until Riley did. They were halfway to her house before he finally spoke.

"You know it doesn't have to go on like this."

Zandy nodded. "I know. What's sad to realize is that you know full well what you're doing to my family and all because of your lustful inclinations. How do you feel when you sit down to your five-course dinners knowing that because of your cruelty, my brothers and sister are going to bed hungry?" Zandy had stopped walking by this time. The truth was she wasn't feeling very capable of continuing without a rest. Thinking back, it'd been over three days since she'd eaten much of anything.

"You should ask yourself that question, Zandy."

Zandy felt herself grow faint. *Please, God,* she prayed silently, *don't let me faint in front of this man.* She immediately reached out for the basket, and Riley didn't stop her from taking it.

"You don't look well. When was the last time you ate?" Riley questioned her sternly.

"That's none of your concern. I'm quite well, thank you." Zandy turned to continue toward home, only to find Riley keeping pace with her.

"What about your stepmother? She can't be doing too well by now. My doctor tells me she would have used up the last of her medicine a week ago."

Zandy's shocked expression bothered Riley but, for the life of him, he couldn't make himself give in. "What a deplorable man you are! Will you deny us the pine box to bury our dead as well?"

Riley was the one notably surprised this time. "No one has died, yet." His words weren't in character with his brazen attitude earlier. "No one needs to die, Alexandra."

"No one needs to go hungry, either. I doubt in all seriousness," Zandy said as she reached her yard, "that even if I gave in to you that my family would be provided for. You have no heart, Riley Dawson. People like you don't keep their word because they have no values, no principles. May God have mercy on your soul, Riley."

Riley stood in silence watching as Zandy made her way into the house. Somehow he'd thought the whole matter would have ended weeks ago. He'd misjudged the stuff of which Alexandra Stewart was made.

As if predestined by Riley's words, Ruth Stewart fell gravely ill. Zandy took over the chores of caring for Molly and even began to wean her on cornbread, brown sugar, and canned milk.

"Poor little one," Zandy said as she held the crying infant who burrowed her face eagerly against Zandy's breast, hoping to find something other than the calico blouse. Ruth had been too sick to even nurse Molly, and the child was suffering. It served to remind Zandy that if she would only give in to Riley's deviant proposal, Molly and the rest would have what they needed to sustain life.

As Zandy spooned small bits of mushed cornbread into Molly's mouth, she began to contemplate accepting Riley's demands. *Lord, I know that that kind of life isn't right, but neither is it right for a baby to go hungry or for a woman to die from lack of medicine. God, it really is my fault, and the answer is so simple. I know it would only hurt me, but right now everyone is hurting.* Zandy looked down at her baby sister and felt the tears slide down her cheeks to fall upon the baby's face.

Suddenly, Zandy felt that she knew what she had to do. Finishing Molly's feeding, Zandy bundled the baby up and took off in the direction of the Dawson mansion.

Zandy wondered silently what Riley would think when he saw her coming up his pathway. Her dark blue skirt had been altered to fit her better but the blouse still looked two sizes too large. Zandy knew he'd be very much aware of her appearance, but she felt it her mission to deliver into Riley's hands, or at least bring to his attention, the young baby that he was responsible for starving.

As she approached the cultivated gardens that surrounded the mansion, Zandy had second thoughts about her plan. Before she could turn around though, Mike Muldair met her on the path.

"And what'll ye be doing here today, lassie?" he questioned in his heavy Irish brogue.

"I need to see Mister Dawson," Zandy replied while shifting Molly to her other hip. Molly was looking around at the brilliantly colored flowers, totally oblivious to her older sister's discomfort.

"Why would ye be needin' to do that? Mister Dawson is a mite busy," Mike said as he stroked his red beard.

"I don't care. Tell him Alexandra Stewart is here to see him. I'm certain that he'll want to talk to me."

"Alexandra Stewart? Well, why didn't ye say so?" Mike said as he motioned Zandy to follow. "Come along, lass. Ye'll not be wanting to keep the man waiting."

Zandy said nothing but followed the Irishman through the gardens and up the stairs to the mansion's veranda. "I'll wait here," Zandy said firmly. "You tell Mister Dawson that I'll see him out here."

Mike Muldair looked surprised and chuckled to himself. Then, turning to open the large double doors, he spoke to himself, "And did ye hear her? Tell Mister

Dawson that I'll be seein' him out here. Imagine that."

He was still talking to himself as he disappeared out of sight, and Zandy couldn't suppress a shudder as she considered what she was doing.

When Riley appeared in the doorway, Zandy noted his casual attire. She'd never seen Riley out of his finely tailored suits, but standing here in a simple cotton shirt and black pants, Zandy could almost forget he was the high and mighty man who controlled Dawson, Colorado, with an iron fist.

"And to what do I owe the pleasure?" Riley said as he leaned back against the door frame.

Zandy was at a loss for words. What had she planned to say? Molly started to fuss and pull at Zandy's hair. "I thought," Zandy said slowly, "that you should see my little sister. I wanted you to know that your actions are grieving even a helpless infant, not to mention four little boys who don't understand why they can't eat regular meals like their friends do."

"I see," Riley said as he came forward and reached out to smooth back the strand of Zandy's hair that Molly had pulled loose. "And you thought that somehow this would make me change my mind?"

"I hoped that you would do the decent thing and help them by giving my father his job back and allowing us credit at the stores. My stepmother is dying, Riley, and you've got to allow the doctor to help her."

Riley felt a moment of discomfort as Molly reached out to grab his finger. He quickly pulled his hand back, making Molly think he was playing with her. Her gurgling baby sounds made Riley smile.

"She'll be dead in no time at all," Zandy said matter-of-factly. "A baby can't live long without food or without a mother."

Riley looked thoughtful for a moment. "I'm sure that is true. I will give you food for your family and milk for your little sister." Zandy felt a wave of hope wash over her weak frame, but it was short lived as Riley continued, "just as soon as you take your sister home and move into my house. I will send Mike to personally deliver ten dollar's worth of groceries to your family. I will also send the doctor with the medicine that your stepmother needs."

"You're a ruthless man, Mister Dawson," Zandy said and turned to leave.

"And you are a selfish, spoiled young woman. Your loved ones are hurting, suffering from hunger and sickness because your pride and selfish morals won't allow you to help them. After they're dead, Alexandra, do you think people will praise your piety? Will they erect a memorial to the one person who could have saved her family, but vainly chose to ignore their need?"

"Vanity has nothing to do with this," Zandy said as tears welled in her eyes. "I believe God has a plan for His children, and I believe in His word, the Bible. What you propose to me is against everything that I hold dear and true. I will never be willing to throw those beliefs aside."

"Then their blood will be on your head," Riley said and left Zandy to contemplate his words.

six

Mountain summer was a glorious time but its pleasures were lost on Zandy. The quaking aspen trees whispered a Colorado melody, and all that passed beneath their pulsating boughs were captivated, if not hypnotized, by the sound.

Zandy remembered when Pastor Brokamp had told her that the aspen were quaking because Christ passed beneath one on His way to Calvary. Still others told Zandy it was because the cross itself was made of aspen wood. Either way, Zandy had come to find a certain comfort in the sound.

The one ray of hope was that the garden plot was just starting to provide food for the Stewart family. Zandy was more than happy to labor long hours in the garden in order to provide the bounty that God grew there. Somehow, it made her feel vindicated and less responsible for her family's plight.

One evening after a lean supper of vegetable soup, the Stewarts were surprised to find a visitor at their door.

"Pastor Brokamp, please come in," Ruth said as she finished putting the last of the dishes on the shelf.

"I heard that times were difficult for you. We took up a collection and brought you some things. If you'll come outside and help me unload Mabel, I'd be much obliged," Pastor Brokamp announced.

Ruth's face clearly showed the gratitude she felt. "Thanks be to God," she said as she moved with Zandy and Burley toward the door.

"No, Ruth. You just sit. Zandy and I can get whatever Pastor Brokamp has brought us. No sense wearing yourself out when you're just starting to feel better."

Ruth, who'd begun to enjoy a bit of health, nodded. It was as if the warmer, dry mountain air had eased some of her congestion. Zandy believed it was God's response to her faithful obedience. She knew that God wouldn't let them go on being hungry or sick.

Zandy and her father were surprised to find Pastor Brokamp's donkey packed to overflowing. There wasn't even an inch of room for the irritating horseflies to pester the jenny's back.

After they finished helping Pastor Brokamp carry the goods into the house, the preacher offered a prayer for their health and prosperity and took Mabel back down the path to Dawson.

"I've never seen so much food in my life," Ruth began as she sorted through the abundance.

"The store has this much food, Ma," Joshua offered as he helped to put away the cans of fruit and milk.

"This place will look like a store for sure when we get all this food put away," Burley Stewart told his oldest son.

Zandy went to bed that night with a full stomach and a grateful heart. God was so very good to have provided for her loved ones. It only served to confirm that she'd done the right thing by standing up to Riley Dawson.

"Thank You, God," Zandy whispered as she

snuggled down in the covers. Before continuing her prayer, she glanced across the room to see that Joshua and Samuel were already sound asleep. "I just knew that I was doing the right thing. Thank You for giving me a sign of encouragement."

Zandy's hopefulness lasted only until the next day when she found out that Riley Dawson had closed down the church. Pastor Brokamp took the announcement in stride and refused to leave his small cabin. Instead, he announced that anyone who wanted to be his house guest on Sundays would be very welcomed.

Later that morning, Jim Williams appeared at the Stewarts' doorstep to give Zandy a sealed envelope from Riley.

"What does he want?" Zandy said as she looked at the writing on the envelope.

"I don't know. He just called me in and asked me to deliver this to you. He said you were to read it right away. I can't say I was happy to oblige him, but I didn't get much of a choice," Jim said in a rather discouraged tone.

Poor Jim, Zandy thought to herself. If Riley hadn't come along imposing his will upon everyone, Jim might have found a way to marry her. Now, however, Zandy doubted that Jim would ever feel comfortable with her again.

"I'm supposed to get on back to the jail," Jim finally said and turned to leave.

"Jim, I. . . ." Zandy wasn't sure what it was that she wanted to say, but somehow she wished that she could console him.

"There's nothing to say, Zandy. You don't owe me any explanation. I know how demanding Dawson can be. Just be careful."

Zandy was touched by Jim's concern. "I will be." She wanted to say more, but Jim was already headed back to town.

Zandy opened the envelope and read the contents.

I want to see you at the church. Now!
Riley

"Of all the nerve," Zandy said as she opened the lid on the stove and shoved the letter and envelope inside. She poked the letter down into the ashes until it caught fire and burned.

"That's all the attention I'll give you, Mister Riley Dawson," Zandy muttered as she tied her apron on. A wave of ominous guilt washed over her, however, causing her to rethink her words. "Oh, all right," she said as she took off the apron and slammed it down on the table.

Zandy quickly braided her hair into a single plait down the back and tied it with a ribbon. She was glad that Ruth had taken the children visiting for she had no desire to explain to Ruth or her father as to why Riley Dawson would be summoning her. Zandy hated to be so obedient to Riley's request, but there was really nothing to be gained in raising his ire.

She entered the church with a cautious glance. Riley

was nowhere to be seen, so Zandy made her way to the front of the church and took a seat in the family pew.

"You certainly took your time," Riley said as he walked into the church, letting the door close with a resounding bang.

Zandy couldn't suppress a shudder. This was a confrontation she wasn't eager to face. "I came as soon as I could get away," she said, refusing to offer an apology.

Riley walked to the front of the church and took a seat in the pew directly in front of her. "Your Pastor Brokamp made a mistake in crossing me. I've closed the church."

"Yes, I know," Zandy said matter-of-factly.

Riley raised an eyebrow. "You know? My, my, news travels fast in this little town. Do you also know that you're the reason?"

"Me?" Zandy couldn't suppress her surprise.

"Yes. Brokamp brought your family food last night. He knew better. He'd already been to see me about increasing your father's hours at the mine, and I informed him that he should stay out of the matter. He chose not to, and so I closed the church."

"So, once again, because I am being obedient to God and not to Riley Dawson, a good and caring man is being punished. Fair or not fair, Mister Dawson, I find your idea of a good life very strange." Zandy paused to see if Riley might offer some objection and when he didn't, she continued. "You came here offering people happiness, wealth, prosperity, and, in a way, salvation from their miseries. So far you've managed to make yourself the most despised as well as the best-loved man in all of

Dawson. You had the potential to create a dynasty for yourself. You had people eating out of your hand and being happy to do it. Now, you've made a grave mistake. Oh, I realize the masses won't care. They are as you once told me, the godless who would sell their souls for a claim. But, Mister Dawson," Zandy boldly stared Riley in the eye, "the original townsfolk, the ones you made your promises to, they will despise and reject you for harming their pastor and church. You have made a very bad mistake."

Riley studied her seriously for a moment. There was no doubt about it, Alexandra Stewart was an intelligent woman. There was a great amount of truth in what she had to say, and Riley couldn't just ignore it. Perhaps it was time to change tactics. It bore consideration.

"Alexandra, I'm sorry that it was necessary to close the church. I'm even sorry that others are suffering. It was never my intention for anyone to get hurt. I only wanted to treat one extraordinary woman to a very special life. Hurting people and causing folks to suffer was never a part of my plan."

"Then why allow it to continue?" Zandy questioned.

"Because," Riley said with a heavy sigh, "I can't back down now."

"Why? Is your pride really worth the pain you're causing?"

"I'm causing? I'm not the one causing this," Riley could tell by the look on Zandy's face that he wasn't making any more progress than the times before. "I'm not a monster, Alexandra. Why not allow yourself to enjoy my company and the things that I can give you?

You can't be happy with the constant worry of what the winter will bring. You can't expect another collection to come by way of the townspeople."

"The people didn't send us that collection. God did, Riley," Zandy softened her voice. In a way, she felt very sorry for Riley Dawson. He had no way of understanding her faith in God. "God will always take care of His children."

"I don't consider eight people living in a three-room shack, being cared for. Zandy," Riley said using her nickname, "you could live in a mansion, like a queen."

" 'I had rather be a doorkeeper in the house of my God, than to dwell in the tents of wickedness.' That's Psalm 84:10," Zandy said, feeling a need to share her faith with Riley. "The Bible is filled with verses that speak to us of finding value in the simple things of righteous people rather than the wealth and glory of the godless." Suddenly, it seemed so clear to Zandy that what she should have been doing all along was showing Riley the road to salvation.

"Those are just words that poor people comfort themselves with," Riley said, looking slightly disturbed by Zandy's revelation. "How strong will your faith be now that your church is gone?"

"My faith in God doesn't exist simply because a church building opens its doors. My faith in God runs so much deeper," Zandy explained. "Oh, Riley, I wish you could understand. I believe in God and the salvation He's offered me, not because of this building, or Pastor Brokamp, or even my Christian parents. I believe in God because the Bible showed me who He was and why

He cared about me. I accepted His love and repented of my old, sinful ways, and now I have the best that life can possibly offer, all because I have Him."

"So nothing has changed?" Riley questioned, sounding rather awkward.

Zandy smiled, and it disturbed Riley more than he would ever allow himself to realize. "A great deal has changed. I know now why God sent you into my life. Before this moment I was constantly asking God why He would allow such a time of testing, but now I see why. God wants you to know Him, Riley."

Riley tried to chuckle at the words but he had an almost fearful feeling that Zandy was right. "We'll see just how long you maintain this point of view."

"Why, what have you planned for me now?"

"Not so much for you, Zandy, as much as for everyone else," Riley said as he got up. He felt the need to get away from Zandy before her words of God and faith changed his mind and his plans.

"Just what do you mean, Riley?" Zandy said and rushed to his side. When Riley continued to walk down the aisle, Zandy reached out and took hold of his arm.

It was more than Riley had expected, and he quickly turned to pull Zandy into his arms. Their eyes met for only a moment, but a moment was enough. Zandy knew that touching Riley had been the wrong thing and, as Riley's mouth crushed down on her's, Zandy's mind went blank.

When Riley released her, Zandy took a step backward and raised her hand to her mouth. More troubling to her than Riley's kiss was the fact that she wasn't repulsed by it the way she'd hoped she'd be. The look of confusion betrayed her feelings.

"Think about this moment when everyone turns against you because of their losses. Think about it and remember how you feel right this minute." With that Riley was gone, and Zandy was left to regather her wits.

seven

Zandy hadn't long to wait until she understood exactly what Riley Dawson had in mind. Word spread throughout the town about the increased percentage of profits that was to go to Riley's personal bank account. Then, there was the increased cost of goods that arrived weekly through Riley's selected freighters. One by one, every family in Dawson was affected, and when Riley forced more than one family to turn over their property in lieu of credit extended at the various stores in town, the people became enraged.

At the people's request, Riley held an open forum at the town hall. The building was crowded to overflowing with every inch of standing room filled by one body or another. Zandy offered to take the boys back home while Ruth and Burley stayed on but, just as she turned to leave, Jim Williams approached them.

"Mister Dawson says that I'm to make sure you're given a proper place to stand. I'm to escort you to the roped off section at the front."

"But why the special treatment?" Burley questioned.

Zandy felt her heart sink. So this was Riley's retaliation. He planned to publicly humiliate her family. She didn't even hear Jim's reply but simply followed her father and stepmother through the crowd.

How could he be so cruel? Zandy asked herself over

and over. "If he had only been kind," Zandy muttered to herself, "I might have actually fallen in love with him."

"What did you say, Zandy?" Ruth leaned over to ask amidst the din of noise.

Zandy shook her head. "Nothing, Ruth." The fact was her statement startled her in a way that she couldn't explain. Was it true? Could she really have thought herself capable of falling in love with Riley Dawson?

She hadn't any time to consider the matter as Riley approached the front of the room.

"If everyone will quiet down, I'll begin this meeting," Riley shouted above the noise.

An immediate hush fell over the room, and people began to push forward ever so slightly in order to hear whatever might be said.

"I know many of you are unhappy with the new arrangements we've made for your businesses and working hours. I have only one thing to say about the matter. I offered Miss Alexandra Stewart a very tempting proposal, and she rejected me. I suggest if you are unhappy that you take it up with her." Riley stared squarely into Zandy's shocked face. The hurt in her eyes nearly caused him to wince. Why should it bother him that she was upset? He intended to have his own way in this matter and by whatever means it took to accomplish his goal.

Zandy could see the hurtful and angry stares of her neighbors and friends. Even her family looked at her with eyes that questioned Riley's announcement.

"What does he mean, Zandy?" her father asked in a

guarded tone.

"I, uh. . .," Zandy felt at a loss for words. She wanted to cry but wouldn't give Riley the privilege of seeing her break down.

"Let's discuss this at home, Burley," Ruth offered and moved her children out of the roped area.

"What's he talking about, Miss Alexandra? Are you causing us grief just because you don't want to marry Riley Dawson?" someone questioned from the crowd.

Someone else joined in with their opinion. "I don't reckon to see my kids going without like your brothers and sister. Just marry the man and let us be."

A rousing cry of agreement came out of the crowd, and Zandy's eyes narrowed slightly as she squared her shoulders and gave Riley Dawson a look that made him think better of having crossed her.

Riley was still contemplating his action after the crowd had dispersed and the Stewarts had gone home. Why had he done it? He knew he'd hurt her and that was never his real intention. Of course, he thought as he walked to his mansion on the hill, he'd never expected her to endure for so long. He'd never in his life had the slightest trouble getting his way with women, but then he'd never met a woman of virtue that interested him. But, that was before Alexandra Stewart had come into his life.

Even the children were quiet as the Stewart family entered their little house. A deluge of painful accusations and suspicious eyes had followed them all the way home, and when they had closed the door behind them,

Burley told the boys to go to the back room and play.

"It appears we need to talk, Zandy," Burley said as he planted his large frame on a kitchen chair.

Ruth left the room only long enough to put Molly down for a nap and soon joined Burley at the table.

Zandy remained standing, feeling as though she were being tried in court for a crime she had not committed. Silently she prayed that she might be able to say the right thing.

"Is what Mr. Dawson said true? Did you reject him?" Burley questioned.

"Yes, but—" Zandy started to explain but her father cut her off.

"You rejected him even knowing what he would do to your family and the town?" Burley asked and the anger in his voice surprised Zandy.

"I didn't feel his proposal was in keeping with the Word of God," Zandy declared, hoping that the words would speak for themselves.

"So you took it upon yourself to interpret the Bible and bring down grief upon your family. Did it ever occur to you that perhaps this punishment came because you weren't doing the will of God?" Burley questioned, and Zandy felt the color drain from her face.

"Pa, you don't understand. Riley Dawson isn't all that he seems."

"So now you're an authority on the Bible and on men."

"Now, Burley, don't get so upset. I'm sure Zandy has a good reason for turning away a fine man like Riley Dawson. Perhaps she just needs time to get to know him."

Burley pounded his fist down on the table causing both Zandy and Ruth to jump. "Those little ones in the back room went hungry because of you. You had it in your means to save them from their pain, and yet you allowed it to go on. How could you be so cruel? I didn't raise you to be so selfish."

Zandy stared open-mouthed at her father and stepmother. Nobody cared what her reasoning was. Nobody cared that Riley wanted a mistress and not a wife. Perhaps they would have if she'd been allowed to explain herself but, instead, her father clearly wanted no explanation.

"I have to face the people of this town every day. Why, the church even took up a collection for this family. Those people must feel like complete fools now," Burley surmised. "I don't understand you. I would think you'd be grateful for the promising life that Riley Dawson could offer."

"Zandy," Ruth said softly, trying to balance out the boisterous voice of her father, "what is it that troubles you so about marrying Riley?"

Zandy sat down across from her parents in a most dejected manner. What could she say? Should she tell her father about Riley's real request? What could possibly be gained if she told her father that he wanted her to live in sin with him? Either her father wouldn't care in order to save the rest of the family and town, or he'd be so angry that he'd give Riley a piece of his mind and lose his job.

"Your ma asked you a question. Are you going to

answer her?" Burley said in a calmer tone. Ruth always had that effect on Burley and now, as Ruth clasped her hand in his, Zandy knew that he would relax a bit.

"I don't love Riley Dawson," Zandy stated sadly.

"Love? Is that what this is all about?" Zandy's father questioned in disbelief. "What about love for your brothers and sister? What about love for your ma who can't get the medicine she needs? I think you'd best spend some time in prayer and reconsider what sacrificial love is all about."

"Zandy, people don't always love each other the way storybooks tell it. You learn to love, though. I think you could learn to love Riley and have a happy life as his wife," Ruth said in an almost pleading tone.

The word "wife," cut Zandy like a knife. She wanted to scream that he doesn't want a wife but instead she remained silent. Only God knew the truth—God and Riley Dawson.

Later that day, when Zandy was working in the garden, Jim Williams appeared out of nowhere. "Care if I hang around a minute?" Jim asked, cautiously.

"No, I guess not," Zandy replied in just as guarded a tone.

"I thought maybe you could use a friend about now," Jim said as he leaned against the crude fencing that lined the front of the property.

"I guess I could at that," Zandy said as she straightened up from pulling onions. "I figured you'd be just as angry at me as everyone else is."

"I'm not mad, Zandy. I guess I just wonder why you don't want to marry Riley. I mean, I know that you aren't seeing anybody, and it just seems like an awful good life to offer a woman. If I had that kind of money, I know I wouldn't waste any time at all in finding me a good wife."

Zandy smiled. Riley had the entire community exactly where he wanted them. They all presumed from his statement that he was doing an honorable, maybe even romantic thing and that Zandy considered herself above the matter or, at best, disinterested in the comfort.

"Just remember, Jim," Zandy finally said, "things aren't always what they seem. You mustn't judge me too harshly."

"I wasn't trying to judge you at all. Frankly, I'm happy that you don't want to marry him. I just wish I could marry you instead. But the truth is, Riley said if I spend any more time with you, he'd fire me."

"I'm sorry, Jim," Zandy said and gathered her gardening tools. "You'd probably better leave before someone sees you here and reports it back to Riley. I don't want anybody to suffer any more because of me."

"I'm not really worried," Jim said, but Zandy knew it was a lie because his eyes continued to dart from side to side as if he were watching for Riley.

"You may not be, but I am. I'm very worried. I'm not sure where all this is leading, but I don't want you involved."

"I hope you know that I'll always care about you," Jim stated softly.

Zandy smiled again. He was so young and handsome and very naive about the power behind Riley Dawson. He shouldn't have come at all, Zandy thought to herself.

"I'm glad that you do, Jim. Thank you." With those few words, Zandy didn't even wait for his response but went quickly into the house.

As Zandy closed the door behind her, she could hear her stepmother still trying to soothe her father's worried mind. The boys were beginning to raise a ruckus in the back room, and Molly was fussing to be fed.

Leaning against the door, Zandy breathed a prayer, "Father, I know that I'm not to disobey my father, and I know that I mustn't dishonor Your Word. Please help me, Lord, to know what to do, Amen." Zandy sighed and put the tools away. It was going to be a long summer.

eight

Day after day, Ruth and Burley went out of their way to ignore Zandy in hopes that she'd make the right choice and marry Riley Dawson.

More than once, Zandy had lain awake in her bed, hearing her father and stepmother talking in hushed whispers about what they would do when the food ran out. Zandy always felt as though she'd had the wind knocked out of her when her father would say that he didn't know what had gotten into Zandy.

Zandy knew they still cared about her, but it was a fine line that she had to walk in order to keep the subject of Riley Dawson from entering the brief bits of conversation that they had at mealtime.

One morning as Burley was leaving for the mines, Zandy happened to be sitting on the front door stoop contemplating the mess she found herself in.

"What are you doing out here?" her father asked as he stepped past Zandy and paused directly in front of her.

"I was just thinking about when I was a little girl. You know, before Ma died." Her father nodded but said nothing. Zandy sighed. "I was so sure that we'd always live in the same house, do the same things, be the same people. I never thought things would change so much."

"Me neither," he admitted sadly and placed a hand on

Zandy's shoulder. "I know things are difficult right now, but I want you to know that I'll never stop loving you."

Zandy needed so much to hear those words. She felt a tear slide down her cheek as she leaned her face to touch his hand and whispered, "I love you too, Pa."

The moment was far too brief and then, without another word, her father walked out the gate and down the path to work. Zandy hugged herself tightly, wishing that the feeling of warmth could go on forever, but a chilling reminder of Riley Dawson haunted her mind. Hours later, Zandy was to remember the moment as one of the most precious in her life.

Most of her days passed in monotonous routine, but this day was different. Without warning, the silence of the day was broken. The loud explosion, followed by the eerie blast of the mining whistle in midday, could only mean one thing—there had been an accident!

Zandy looked up at the same time Ruth did, wondering silently if it would be their family member who had been hurt. Ruth gave Zandy a guarded look. She'd done her best to keep an air of harmony in the house, but her own heart was well tested in light of her children's going without the things they needed. Now, it was only a matter of time before they would learn whether or not Burley was involved in the mining accident.

Zandy opened the front door and looked down the pathway, hoping and praying that her father was safe. Minutes ticked by and, after fifteen minutes had passed, Zandy decided she could wait no longer.

"I'm going to the mine to see what happened," she said as she folded her apron and placed it on the table.

Ruth only nodded.

Zandy was just reaching for the door when she heard the commotion on the path below. Her heart sunk, and a lump fixed itself in her throat. She dared a look at her stepmother to find tears forming in her eyes.

"Not Burley," Ruth whispered, and her hand flew to her mouth to stifle a cry.

A man came rushing ahead of the others to warn Zandy and Ruth to make a place ready.

"He's hurt pretty bad, Missus Stewart," the man said apologetically. "He drilled into a missed hole."

Zandy cringed, knowing only too well what that meant. Missed holes were cavities that had been packed with dynamite but hadn't exploded as expected. Her father would have ignited enough spark while drilling the heavy rock face to set off the unexploded dynamite. In turn, the explosion would have torn the drill operator apart. If they were bringing him home, however, he must still be alive.

"Have they sent for the doctor?" Ruth questioned and began to cough. The consumption was now active again and giving her a great amount of trouble.

"Uh. . .no, ma'am," the man grew quite uncomfortable. "The doc won't come here unless Mister Dawson gives his approval."

Ruth stopped dead in her tracks. She turned with accusing eyes to face Zandy and, for once in her life, Zandy felt anger directed toward her from her stepmother. The look really said it all, and Zandy wanted to look away, but couldn't.

"Do you mean to tell me that my husband is going to be denied a doctor?" Ruth asked the man, all the while looking at Zandy.

"Sorry, ma'am. The men are nearly here, you'd best make the bed ready."

Ruth began to cry, which only aggravated the cough. "I'll pull down the covers," she managed to say.

"I'll help you," Zandy offered.

Ruth turned on her heel and held Zandy at arm's length. "There's only one way you can help. I think you know exactly what that is."

Zandy had no time to reply as the men burst through the door, bearing the stretcher that held her father.

"Oh, Pa," Zandy cried as she caught sight of her father's bloodied body. He was mercifully unconscious and, for all intents and purposes, looked dead.

Zandy tore out of the house on a dead run to the Dawson mansion. Riley just had to listen to reason. He couldn't be so heartless as to refuse a dying man care. Reason eluded Zandy as she flew across the garden path and, without so much as a knock, burst through the doors to the mansion.

"Riley!" she screamed. Tears were flowing down her face, and her hair fell wildly about her shoulders. "Riley Dawson, I demand to see you now!"

Riley stepped from behind double oak doors with a stunned expression on his face. When he saw how upset Zandy was, he crossed the room in several quick strides. "What is it?"

"My father has been blown up! You must send the

doctor to my house," Zandy said as she gripped Riley's arms tightly.

The touch was almost more than Riley could stand, but he did nothing to remove her hands. His real thought was to pull her into his arms and comfort her. Zandy looked so scared and upset that Riley very nearly lost his resolve. His heart cried out to him to be merciful, but his mind told him this was the very chance for which he had waited.

"Alexandra," he began.

"Don't Alexandra me," Zandy said as she dropped her hands. "Don't tell me anything except that you're going to send the doctor to my father."

"I can't," Riley said, and then bit his tongue to keep from taking it back.

Zandy shocked them both by pounding her fists against Riley's chest. "You brute! You monster! You don't care about anything but having your own way. My father is dying, and you don't care."

"You know what I'll expect in return if I send the doctor to your father," Riley said as he took hold of Zandy's wrists.

Zandy fought against his hold, all the while sobbing until the tears came in a wave of hysteria. "He'll die! He'll die! Don't you understand? You have women in town that can satisfy your lustful desires, but my father is going to die if the doctor doesn't come to him now! Please, Riley," Zandy stopped abruptly. "Please don't let him die," she managed between sobs.

Riley released her arms and pulled her against his chest. He couldn't bear the pain in her eyes. "Hush, you're making this much too difficult. Everything is going to be all right."

Zandy allowed Riley to stroke her hair and hold her. She couldn't explain why she wasn't repulsed by the action, nor why she found comfort in it, but then her mind was beyond rational thought, she reasoned.

For several minutes they stood in the vestibule of the Dawson mansion, while Zandy's tears played themselves out against Riley's broad chest. Zandy felt too exhausted to move, and yet she knew that every passing minute might be the determining factor as to whether her father lived or died.

"I know you aren't a bad man, Riley," Zandy said as she pulled away slowly. She dried her eyes with the back of her sleeve. "I don't understand why you've chosen the path you have. Maybe you didn't have good folks to bring you up like I did. Maybe you've had a falling out with God and feel like He's deserted you. I just don't know, but I do feel strongly that you aren't really enjoying this any more than I am. It's become a matter of pride, and your pride will eventually break you."

Riley pushed his hands deep in his pockets to keep from reaching out and pulling Zandy back into his arms. He looked at the young woman before him, the red-rimmed eyes, the wild hair, and in his mind he felt something he'd never before felt for a woman—genuine compassion.

"You're right, Alexandra," Riley spoke softly. "I'm not enjoying this at all."

"Then why not give in and end it?"

Riley gave a stilted laugh, "I suppose because I've always mastered my destiny, and I'm not about to have someone else do it for me now."

"But God masters everyone's destiny, Riley," Zandy said, momentarily forgetting that her father lay dying. "You don't have control over anything at all, Riley. God does."

"God certainly didn't keep your father from getting hurt in the mines."

"There is a purpose for everything," Zandy said and suddenly realized the truth of her own words. "Even this has a purpose."

"A purpose that might cause you to give in and join me here?" Riley questioned.

Zandy stepped back, shaking her head. "You can have 'most any other woman Riley. Please don't force me to give myself over to be your mistress in order to save my father's life. It just isn't that simple. Court me or marry me, but don't ask me to shame myself before my God."

The words shocked Riley. Would she actually be willing to marry him? "If God is the way you say He is, knowing everything and all, then He'd know that becoming my mistress wasn't your idea. He'd know and He wouldn't blame you. So why concern yourself with saying that you'd shame yourself? You know full well the responsibility would be mine, and I don't care."

Zandy swallowed hard. Riley made it sound so simple. Wasn't it true that God would indeed know the difference? Wouldn't it be easy to just give in and deal with the consequences later?

A picture of her father, bleeding and unconscious, came to mind. Was one sacrifice worth the other? Zandy turned to leave, and Riley couldn't help but follow after her. Before he could speak, Zandy stopped at the door.

"I'm praying for you, Riley. I have been ever since the first night I met you. Praying that you'd be the salvation for our town that we needed, praying that God would open your eyes to your willful and sinful spirit, and praying that God would allow you to find mercy upon the people in this town and me." Zandy said the words in such a way that Riley felt completely engulfed by each and every one. "My father's life is in God's hands. That's something I forgot before coming up here. I guess my fears got the best of me, but I want you to know that I'm going to keep on praying for you, Riley. I know there is good inside you, and I know that God can deal with you and bring out that good."

With those final words, Zandy stepped out into the night and hurried toward the path that would lead home.

Riley could only stare after her. Why had her words so disturbed him?

"Such foolish feminine notions," Riley muttered as he watched Zandy disappear from view. But as he closed the door, his heart and mind were at war for control, and Riley silently wished he'd never come to Dawson, Colorado.

nine

When Zandy walked back into her house, she could hear the commotion of the men as they tried to help Ruth in the back room. Zandy quickly put a kettle of water on to boil and found an old sheet that she could tear into bandages.

"God, please help me. I need to do my very best in order to help my father and stepmother. Please guide me and help me," Zandy said the words but, in the back of her mind, she felt the nagging doubt of faltering faith.

She wanted so much to believe, and yet never had her faith been tested so severely. Surely the Word of God was true. It just had to be true and Zandy had to be able to trust that God would deliver her from the pain and confusion.

Riley's words came back to haunt her, though, and Zandy wondered silently if she shouldn't be the one to give up and accept Riley's proposition. At least everyone in town would be treated better, and she felt confident that Riley would send the doctor to help.

Hearing her father cry out in pain brought Zandy rudely back to reality. She was so tired and so confused. What seemed simple and orderly in the printed words of the Bible somehow didn't seem to fit the lawless life of Dawson, Colorado.

Ruth's ceaseless crying, mingled with the violent

coughing spasms, sent Zandy to the door. If the only way she could get help was to offer herself to Riley Dawson, then she'd call Riley the victor and give in. Opening the door, Zandy was shocked to find the doctor on the other side.

"I was sent to care for your father," the doctor said as he entered the room.

Zandy breathed a prayer of thanksgiving. "Please hurry! He's right back there."

Zandy brought the doctor to her father's bedside and cast Ruth a glance as the doctor ordered everyone from the room.

Ruth's eyes held gratitude as well as pain. Zandy knew she was suffering for both her husband and herself. Zandy tried to look hopeful as she looked from her father's mangled body to her stepmother's face.

"Bring me some hot water," the doctor ordered as he went quickly to the business of caring for Burley.

"I'll get it," Zandy said as she hurried from the room.

She pulled down the wash basin, filled it with water from the stove, and rushed back to her father's bedside.

"Could've been much worse," the doctor said as he stripped pieces of clothing away from Burley's chest. Ruth clung tightly to her husband's hand, as the doctor began to wash away the rock and bits of dirt that had embedded themselves in Burley's skin.

Just then one of the neighbor women came to announce that she was taking the children to her house. Zandy refused to look into the accusing eyes of the woman who, up until a few days ago, had been a good friend. Ruth offered her thanks and quickly turned her attention back to Burley.

"Hand me that bottle," the doctor said and pointed Zandy in the direction of a corked blue bottle.

Zandy quickly complied and watched as the doctor generously poured the contents on Burley's wounds. "This will fight proud flesh," the doctor said, referring to the dreaded blood poisoning that had caused more than one to lose a limb or die.

Ruth began to cough so violently that Zandy noticed the blood on the back of her sleeve when Ruth lowered her hand from her face.

"Get her to bed and give her this," the doctor said and handed Zandy a packet of powder. "Mix it in a glass of water and have her drink it."

"I'm not. . .," Ruth sputtered and coughed, trying hard to protest leaving her husband's side.

"You're going to bed, or I'll not do another thing to help this man," the doctor said sternly. "I won't save his life only to have him wake up to find his wife dead."

Ruth went begrudgingly with Zandy but once she was seated on one of the beds in the boys' room, she nearly collapsed. Zandy brought her the medicine and helped hold Ruth steady as she drank the contents.

"Tastes awful," Ruth said as she handed Zandy the empty glass. Zandy couldn't help but notice the gritty residue in the bottom of the glass.

"I can well imagine," Zandy said as she placed the glass on the bedside table.

Easing Ruth back into the bed, Zandy was surprised to find her stepmother clinging tightly to her arm. "Zandy, I'm so sorry," she said between coughs. "Please forgive me for the way I've acted. Please."

Zandy smiled and pulled the covers over Ruth's bone-thin body. "There's nothing to forgive. I love you, Ruth. You've been a dear mother to me. You just rest, and I'll see to Pa."

Ruth nodded, and Zandy was relieved to find that Ruth was well on her way to losing consciousness.

"What did you give my stepmother?" Zandy questioned as she rejoined the doctor.

"Sleeping powder. I knew it would ease the cough and put her out of her misery for a short time. I can better tend her later. Your pa is cut up pretty bad, but I think he'll be all right. I'm going to stay with him through the night, so you might as well get some rest."

Zandy shook her head. "There is something I need to do. Will you be all right if I leave the house? I want to tell the children that things are going well, and I want to . . .," her voice fell silent. She didn't want to tell anyone that she intended to go and thank Riley for saving her father's life.

"Things are well under control," the doctor said. "You go and do what you must."

Zandy quickly made her way to the neighbor's house, and after assuring the children that things were going to be all right, she made her way to the Dawson mansion.

Her entrance into the house was a far cry from her earlier one. She waited patiently at the door until the butler appeared to admit her.

"Please tell Mr. Dawson that I need to speak with him," Zandy requested.

"The hour is quite late, Miss. . .," the butler began, but

Riley's appearance in the hallway ended anything further that he might have said.

"It's all right," Riley said and waved the butler away. "Come on in, Alexandra. I was expecting you." His dark eyes pierced her soul.

"I wanted to thank you for sending the doctor. My father is doing much better, and the doctor gave my mother something to help her sleep."

"Why don't you come on into the library with me? I was just taking some coffee and cakes. You look like you could use some refreshments," Riley offered, and his casual generosity surprised Zandy.

"I can't stay long, but it does sound good," she found herself saying without thought. She allowed Riley to lead her through the double oak doors that opened into the library. The room was glorious, and Zandy thought that she'd never seen anything quite so beautiful.

"Please, sit," Riley said as he pointed to a blue high-backed chair. Zandy did as he directed and accepted a cup of coffee in a fine bone china cup. Riley placed the delicate saucer on the table beside her chair and brought her another small plate with several miniature cakes. It all seemed so pleasant.

Zandy took a drink and grimaced at the bitter taste. She'd never acquired a fondness for coffee, especially without benefit of cream and sugar.

Riley took the seat across from her without noticing her expression. "So, tell me about your father. What did the doctor say?"

"The doctor said it could have been much worse. He thinks Pa will make it. He also promised to look in on

Ruth," Zandy said and took another drink. "I can't thank you enough, Riley. I knew you had a streak of good in you, and I knew that God wouldn't let me down."

Riley tried not to frown, but the look crossed his face before he could hide it. "I'm glad he's going to make it."

Zandy felt the tension ease from her body as she allowed herself to relax, knowing that her father was receiving the best of care. "I really should get back," Zandy said as she yawned. "I'm totally spent, but I had to thank you." Taking one final drink from the cup, Zandy noticed the gritty residue in the bottom of the cup. A feeling of dread filled her as she struggled to focus on the cup. "I need to go home," she said as she got to her feet and tried to balance herself.

"Sit down, Alexandra," Riley ordered. "Sit down before you fall down."

Zandy tried to put the coffee cup on the table but missed, and the clattering sound seemed to reverberate in her ears. It was abundantly clear to her that Riley had drugged her coffee.

"Why?" she asked with sad accusation in her eyes. "Why?"

Riley put his cup down and stood up slowly. "Because you wouldn't listen to reason."

"I came here to thank you," Zandy said in a slurring manner. "I thought you were being kind. I. . .," Zandy swayed and gripped the side of her chair.

Riley stepped forward to take hold of her, but Zandy pushed him away and nearly fell backward. "Leave me alone," she struggled to say. Her words sounded foreign to her. "Dear God, help me," Zandy worked hard to retain her balance and remember what she wanted to pray. "For he shall give his angels charge over thee, to keep thee in all thy ways." Zandy quoted from Psalm 91:11, trying to plead with God for protection. "Keep me, Lord. Save me from Riley Dawson's lustful passions."

The words were barely audible, but Riley recognized them easily. It was as if his ears alone could make out each and every word with total clarity. She was praying as she had said she'd done before.

Zandy felt herself pitch forward and knew that she couldn't help herself. Riley's strong arms reached out and took hold of her shoulders.

"I can give you a wonderful life, Alexandra," Riley tried to salve his conscience. He'd thought this would be a simple task, but it was proving to be more and more difficult.

Zandy's head fell forward as she struggled to stay awake. She snapped her head back and opened her eyes wide as if it would help her to see clearly.

"I'm still not willing," she said, delivering the words in all their simplicity to Riley's heart. "Not willing, just drugged."

The words hit their mark. She wasn't willing. Once again it was just a matter of Riley's forced will. Hadn't he told her that he'd wait forever for her heart to be willing?

Ever so gently he reached up to push back a loose strand of dark hair. "You are so beautiful. Why can't you understand?"

Zandy felt herself falling; she could no longer stand. It would only be a matter of seconds and she'd be unconscious. "Save me, God," she murmured and fell against Riley.

Riley easily lifted her into his arms. What should he do now, he wondered. He knew what he'd planned to do, but now found his selfish desires impossible to satisfy. Never in his life had his conscience so bothered him.

"Mrs. Malloy!" Riley called out for his housekeeper. Even at this late hour, Riley knew that the older woman would be within earshot.

True enough the grandmotherly woman came from seemingly out of nowhere to answer her employer's call. "Yes?"

"I'm afraid Miss Stewart has collapsed in exhaustion. Will you help me put her to bed?" Riley asked as he cradled Zandy in his arms.

"Of course, sir. I'll pull down the covers in the Blue Room," Mrs. Malloy stated in a refined manner. Taking the lead, Mrs. Malloy went up the stairs ahead of Riley.

"Not willing," Zandy whispered in her nightmarish state of mind. She was dreaming and all around her were people condemning her for not helping her family.

Her words were only loud enough for Riley to hear, and he grimaced at the impact of what he'd done. "I know, Alexandra. I know."

Mrs. Malloy had pulled back the covers and sheets on a huge canopy bed and turned to Riley, "Shall I bring her one of my nightgowns?"

Riley shook his head. "No. We'll just leave her dressed," he said as he deposited her on the bed. "Can you watch over her through the night?"

"Certainly," Mrs. Malloy replied. "I'll go get my knitting and sit right here."

"Thank you. You may of course take tomorrow off to replenish your rest."

"Thank you, sir. I'll be right back."

With that the older woman left the room leaving Riley alone with Zandy. Riley looked at the sleeping figure. She looked so young there on the huge bed. Why did the term "sacrificial lamb" come to mind?

Gently he reached over to cover her. "Don't hurt me," Zandy murmured in her sleep. "Please, don't hurt me."

Riley felt a stab of guilt. He'd caused her such fear and pain. How could he live with the person he'd become?

"Shhh," Riley whispered as he leaned down. "I won't hurt you."

Just then Mrs. Malloy returned, and Riley took the opportunity to escape the obvious reminder of his deception. Taking himself to his own bedroom, Riley slammed the door and began to pace.

"I don't know why this has to be so hard. Why did she have to say no, and why did she have to say the things she said?" Riley muttered as he paced.

He went to pour himself a drink, then thought better of it and threw the whole bottle, along with the glass, into the fireplace. "I don't care what she said. I am no good, and there's no way I can be redeemed. I'm too far gone." Riley said as he threw himself down into a chair.

The silent reminder of Zandy's prayers came back to haunt him. She'd actually prayed for him as well as for protection from him. How could she do that? How could she care enough to ask her God to change him? And why did she have to see through his façade of ruthlessness and know that there was gentleness and compassion buried deep inside?

Well into the night, Riley contemplated his actions and Zandy's words. His mind had been so fixed on having her, and now she lay helpless in his house but, for reasons beyond Riley's understanding, he couldn't touch her.

ten

Sleep eluded Riley and, when the clock in the hall chimed four, he could no longer stand the solitude. Quietly, he slipped into the Blue Room where Mrs. Malloy sat dozing beside Zandy's sleeping form.

The housekeeper stirred, and Riley moved to where she sat. "You go on to bed. I'll sit with her now," Riley ordered.

"Are you certain, sir?"

"Yes, very much so," Riley said, never taking his eyes from Zandy.

He took the seat that Mrs. Malloy vacated and shook his head when she asked him if he'd like her to bring coffee. When the housekeeper was finally gone, Riley leaned forward and put his head in his hands.

His plan had seemed so simple. So why had everything gone so wrong? Why, when a beautiful woman like Alexandra Stewart lay just inches away, was he suddenly unable to carry through with his plan?

She'd prayed for him.

Why had she prayed for him? He didn't deserve her kindness or her prayers. She was so pure, and Riley knew there wasn't another woman like her in all of Dawson.

"What have I done?" he questioned aloud.

In her mind, Zandy heard the voice and wondered

where it had come from. She felt rested and wonderful but, when she opened her eyes, her heart sank. Overhead was a canopy of starched white lace. This was definitely not her home.

She sat up with a start and was further shocked to find Riley Dawson watching her from a chair beside the bed.

"Why am I here? What have you done?" she questioned.

"I was just asking myself the same question," Riley mused. "You spent the night here after you collapsed."

Zandy's mouth dropped open. Then suddenly the memory of the drugged coffee returned to her mind. "Oh, no! This can't be true," Zandy said as she threw the cover back. She was still fully dressed and that offered a bit of comfort to her mind.

Riley sat back in the chair and watched her with a perplexed look on his face. What should he do now? He'd had the opportunity to do her a grave injustice. Would she appreciate the fact that he'd left her alone, or should he allow her to believe the worst?

Zandy sat fixed to her spot. She tried to remember the night before and frowned. "You drugged me."

"Yes," Riley said, offering no apology.

"Why?"

Riley shrugged. "It seemed like a good way to get you relaxed. You know, less inhibited. I thought maybe you were just afraid of what people might say."

Zandy rolled her eyes and sighed. "Well, it would appear, Mister Dawson, that you have created quite an incident here."

"Yes, so it would seem."

"Why are you here?" Zandy questioned.

"I couldn't sleep. I kept thinking of you. I guess just knowing you were so close kept me from being able to relax."

"Are you sure it wasn't your conscience that wouldn't let you rest?" Zandy knew she'd hit a nerve by the look in Riley's eyes.

"I don't know," Riley finally admitted. "I guess I've never had to deal head-on with a woman and her God."

Zandy laughed out loud, and the sound of her laughter was like music to Riley's ears. Why couldn't they spend more time laughing and enjoying each other's company instead of fighting?

"When you deal with me, Riley, you will always have to deal with my God as well. He's always with me, guarding me, protecting me, and loving me."

"He let this happen," Riley stated. "Now your reputation is ruined. People will find out that you spent the night in my house, and it won't matter what room you took residence in. You know the people of this town. They will presume the worst."

Zandy nodded and quietly agreed. "Yes, I suppose that much is true. People are always inclined, or so it would seem, to judge you guilty until they find a reason to do otherwise."

"So why not give in? Why not become my mistress now that everyone will assume you are anyway?" Riley questioned as he crossed his arms.

"I don't care what people think, Riley. I only care about what God knows to be true. He knows the truth. I've done nothing wrong."

"But how can you be sure that I haven't?" Riley questioned seriously.

Zandy smiled. In so many ways, Riley reminded her of one of her little brothers. For all his worldly knowledge and goods, he still lost the meaning of the most important things in life.

"God would never allow you to harm me, Riley," Zandy stated firmly as she threw her legs over the side of the bed. "You see, my faith is firmly planted in Him. Oh, I must admit it hasn't been easy. I very nearly gave in when you wouldn't send the doctor. I kept thinking about what you said and how all of this would be your responsibility. That was true, but God reminded me that He was faithful and that I could trust Him."

"Even if it had cost your father his life?"

"Yes," Zandy nodded and then asked, "Have you had any word on my father?"

"Yes. He's doing fine. Both of your parents are resting comfortably."

"Praise be to God," Zandy said in complete reverence. "Thank you, again for sending the doctor."

"How can you thank me, after what I've done?" Riley questioned as he leaned forward.

Zandy studied him for a moment. From the looks of his rumpled clothes and messy hair, she knew Riley must have slept quite fitfully, if at all. His conscience was bothering him, and it amused her that he finally let his guard down long enough for her to see a bit of the real Riley Dawson.

For reasons beyond Zandy's understanding, she reached out her hand to touch his face. The action surprised Riley, but he didn't move away. "You are so lost, Riley Dawson. My heart cries for you. You are like a little boy who's searching for the safety of home. I know this isn't what you want to hear, but God loves you despite your past and the things you've done. You need to repent and accept His love, because until you do," Zandy said as she looked deep into his brown-black eyes, "you will always be just as unhappy and miserable as you are right this minute."

Riley was stunned into silence by the words of the young woman before him. She didn't talk like a woman who hated him, yet wouldn't he, himself, hate anyone who'd treated him as badly as he'd treated Zandy?

Her touch was so soft, so gentle and loving, and yet Riley knew she would have done the same for anyone. Why did he find himself wishing that she might care singularly for him? Never before had he even considered what she might feel. It was always his own desires that mattered. When she dropped her hand, Riley found its absence almost painful.

The minutes ticked by, and the tension that had existed between them seemed to lessen. It was almost as if the façade of harshness had been destroyed, leaving only the most vulnerable pieces of their lives to show. Riley didn't know why, but he found himself sharing things about his childhood with Zandy.

"My folks were Christians," he said as he eased back into the chair again. "They were killed by Indians when I was back east in college. Nobody really knew why or what had provoked such an action, but nonetheless it happened."

"Then you grew up knowing the truth?"

"That depends on what truth you're speaking of," Riley answered.

"I'm talking about salvation in Christ. Surely your parents did share the Gospel with you."

"I suppose they tried, but I was always an independent thinker. I didn't want to limit myself with religion, so I never paid much attention. When I went back east to college, I fell in with the kind of crowd that kept the same values that I had." Riley paused, contemplating Zandy's long dark hair as it fell around her shoulders framing the thin, pale complexion of her face. How he hated himself for having caused her this pain! "Of course," Riley added, "that meant little or no values at all."

"I can well imagine," Zandy said with a shudder. "Is that when you began to gamble?"

"I suppose that's when I got serious about it. I despised living at college as much as I had living at home, but at least it offered a bit more freedom. I still had to go to chapel on Sunday, but that's where I usually caught up on my reading assignments. I tore off the leather backing to the Bible my parents had given me and covered the book I needed to study from and read my way through the service."

"It's a pity you didn't pay more attention to the inside of the Bible," Zandy mused.

Light was starting to filter in through the drawn curtains, and Zandy suddenly realized she'd better get home before full light or everyone would know where she'd spent the night. "I need to go."

"I know," Riley said and made no move to stop her.

Zandy paused in the doorway and cast a glance at Riley. "I knew there was good in you, Riley. I felt it in my heart."

With those words she was gone, and Riley was left alone with an unfamiliar aching in his heart.

Zandy met the doctor as he was coming from her father's bedside. "You're up mighty early," the doctor said as he quietly closed the door.

"How's my father?" Zandy asked as she pulled on her apron.

"Doing just fine, Miss Stewart. He lost quite a bit of blood, but he's a good strong man. I'm sure he'll do just fine. I'm concerned about your stepmother, however. I've given her enough medicine to last through the week, and then I'll be back."

"What about Riley Dawson?" Zandy couldn't help but question. "He might have other thoughts on the matter."

The doctor frowned. "I gave my life to healing the sick and treating the injured. Riley Dawson has lame ideas about using health as leverage to get his own way. I'll be back, Miss Stewart, rest assured."

"I'm glad," Zandy said with a smile. "Can I fix you some breakfast?"

"No, but thanks anyway. I've got to be getting back to my office," the doctor said as he gathered his things. "If you need me, just send someone."

Zandy nodded and waited until the doctor was on his way before going to check on her father and stepmother.

"Pa?" she whispered as she approached her bandaged

father.

"Is that you, Zandy?"

"Yes," she said as she took hold of his hand.

"Where've you been? I was starting to get worried." Burley Stewart's words were barely audible.

"I'm sorry, Pa. It's a long story. How are you doing?" Zandy asked, hoping he'd let her whereabouts drop for the moment.

"I'm doing better. I thought I was a goner for sure."

"I wish you'd just take us home to Missouri and forget about working at such a dangerous job," Zandy said as she squeezed her father's hand. Ruth's cough from the other room caught her attention.

"I want to check on Ruth," Zandy said as she reluctantly left her father's side.

"Where are the other children?" her father asked weakly.

"Neighbors came and got them last night. I'll fetch them home in a little while. Now, you just rest, and I'll be right back. Do you think you could eat a little something?"

"Not just yet."

Zandy nodded and went to the room where Ruth was. "Ruth?"

"Zandy, are you all right? Where have you been?" Ruth said as she struggled to sit up. "I asked the doctor about you, and he didn't know where you were."

"It's a long story, Ruth," Zandy started, but she could tell by the look in her stepmother's eyes that she wasn't going to get out of it that easily. "I collapsed at the Dawson mansion."

"Collapsed? Are you all right?" Ruth asked a second time and got up from the bed.

"I'm fine, Ruth. God was looking out for me."

"What happened?"

Zandy was grateful for the concern and tenderness that was clearly displayed in her stepmother's face.

Zandy didn't want to lie, but neither did she want to admit that Riley had drugged her. For some reason it seemed important to protect him. "I guess the lack of food and rest caught up with me." It wasn't really a lie, but neither was it the whole truth.

"I'm so sorry, Zandy. I know you've been giving most of your food to the kids, and I appreciate the way you've worked yourself in the garden. Please forgive me for my harshness," Ruth said as she held Zandy close. "I just worry about the little ones so much."

"I know, Ruth. So do I." Zandy hoped fervently it would be an end to the fact that she'd spent the night under Riley's roof, but it wasn't to be so.

A day later, a seething Jim Williams was packing his things when Pat and K.C. came into the room.

"Where ya headed?" K.C. asked as he sat down and put his booted feet up on the chair opposite him.

"I'm leaving this hole," Jim said as he finished stuffing his spare shirt and denims into the bag.

"Why you want to go and do that?" Pat asked as he poured himself some coffee and joined K.C. at the table.

"I just do, that's all," Jim said as he strapped on his gun belt. "I'm going to see the boss man now and get my final pay."

"You ain't leaving because of her, are you?" K.C. questioned with a laugh. "No woman is worth rearranging your life for."

"That's right, Jim," said Pat. "Not even one as pretty as Alexandra Stewart."

"Just shut up," Jim said as he slung his bag over his shoulder.

"You can't still care about her, not after you saw her leave the big house yesterday morning." Pat's words strengthened Jim's resolve to leave.

Jim grimaced and slammed the door behind him. He'd never have believed the gossip in town about Zandy had he not seen her with his own eyes. But, sure enough, what he'd seen, and what all of Dawson was saying, was true—Zandy had spent the night with Riley Dawson.

eleven

A week after the accident, Zandy sat with her parents at the kitchen table. Molly was crawling on the dirt floor while the boys had gone to pick wild raspberries in the hot August sun.

Burley was a quick healer and well on his way to recovering from the wounds he'd received in the mines. The problem, however, was the lack of income. Ruth, too, was looking considerably better and had even managed to work with Zandy in the kitchen. But now they'd joined at the table to contemplate the severe gossip that was spreading through town regarding Zandy's stay at the Dawson mansion.

"Nothing happened," Zandy stated for the second time that morning. "Please understand, it wasn't my idea to stay. I collapsed, and no one gave me a choice."

"I'll have to speak with Dawson," Burley said angrily. "I've had just about as much of this gossip as a body can stand."

"You know, Zandy," her stepmother began, "all of this would fade away if you would just marry the man. The town is simply waiting for Riley to release his hold on their profits and work schedules. So much shouldn't pivot on one woman's choice for a husband, but this time it does. I'm certain that the townspeople would be most forgiving if you would just marry him."

Zandy held her head in her hands. "I can't marry Riley Dawson," was all she managed to whisper.

"You can and you will," her father stated in a demanding tone that he'd never before taken with Zandy.

Zandy's head snapped up. "What do you mean, Pa?"

"I mean that I'm going to go talk to the man today and tell him that you'll be happy to marry him."

"You can't, Pa. You aren't even healed yet. You can't go climbing all over Dawson just to confront Riley," Zandy argued.

"I don't intend to confront the man," Burley stated firmly. "I just want to give him the news he wants to hear."

Zandy sighed and leaned back in her chair. The thin yellow gingham of her well-worn dress reminded her of better days. If only she could take herself back to those times. . .times before Colorado and Riley Dawson.

Ruth placed her hand over Zandy's. "You have to understand that everyone is suffering, and when you marry Riley, everything will go back to the way it was before."

"How can you be so sure?" Zandy questioned.

"What choice do we have?" Ruth asked with tears in her eyes. She reached down and picked up Molly. "Will you see her die of hunger rather than marry a man you don't love?"

Zandy felt a stab of guilt knowing that she'd forced Riley to face the same question. "It's more than that," Zandy protested. "Riley isn't a Christian. You both raised me to marry a man whose faith was the same as mine. A man who'd given his life to God. How can I love someone who doesn't love my God?"

"I don't care if you love him or not," her father said firmly. "I've made up my mind, and you will marry him whether love exists between you or not. And, as far as Riley's salvation is concerned, well, that's a thing between a man and his God." The words certainly didn't sound like Burley Stewart's, but sickness and hunger had done strange things to his heart.

Zandy remained silent, but her eyes were pleading with Ruth to intervene. Ruth only nestled her face against Molly's soft brown hair. Nothing was right.

Just then George came bursting through the door. "Come quick, Zandy. Joshua's fighting with some big boys down by the creek."

Before Burley or Ruth could say a word, Zandy sprang to her feet and flew out the door. She hiked up the long folds of her gingham skirt and ran for all she was worth to Corner Creek.

She could hear the commotion before she could see it and, as she rounded the corner and passed the bridge, Zandy could see that not only Joshua, but Bart and even gentle-spirited Samuel were engaged in a free-for-all with five or six other boys. Rushing headlong into the ruckus, Zandy pulled Joshua out of the grip of a bigger boy.

"Stop this, do you hear me?" Zandy said as she separated the other boys from her brother.

Several of the townspeople had made their way down to the creek and stood off to one side while Zandy tried to sort through the conflict.

"Who started this?" Zandy questioned as she noted Joshua's bloodied nose.

"They did," Samuel spoke up, surprising Zandy. "They said some bad things and wouldn't take 'em back."

"That's right," Joshua said as he pointed his finger to the large boy whom Zandy had pulled from her brother's back. "He said you were a fast woman."

"And that one said you ought to get a job at the saloon," Bart said as he stepped forward in a threatening way toward the indicated boy.

Zandy cast a glance around her to the people who stood just a matter of ten or so feet away. "I see," she said with a guarded reserve to her voice. "People often find it easier to misjudge others than to learn the truth of a matter, boys. The truth is never quite as entertaining as the gossip. These boys aren't to blame, however," Zandy stated loudly enough for all to hear her, "their parents are."

"But Zandy, they was saying real mean things about our family," little George chimed in.

"I know, George, but don't worry about it," Zandy said and lifted her face to meet the people's doubtful stares. "God knows the truth, George, and what these people think is really of little concern to me. Don't let it bother you again, and please, please don't feel you have to defend me. God will do that."

At this most of the onlookers dropped their gazes and refused to meet Zandy's eyes. "Come on, boys, let's get you home and clean you up."

Zandy put her arms around Joshua's shoulders and

gave them a squeeze. "I love you all," Zandy whispered as they climbed the hill. "Thank you for defending me."

Joshua seemed to grow a foot because of his pride of the moment. Bart and Samuel couldn't help but look quite pleased with themselves as well.

Long after everyone had taken themselves to bed, Zandy sat out on the front stoop with her Bible, considering the words her father and stepmother had spoken earlier in the day.

"Father," she whispered to the heavens above her, "I need so much to feel Your touch, to hear Your voice, to know Your love." The wind picked up and the quaking aspen fluttered its rustling melody down the mountainside and across the valley. It sounded so lonely and yet comforting at the same time.

Zandy stared out into brilliantly lit night and watched for some time as a huge full moon crossed the sky. Across the way, an outline of blue spruce and tall ponderosa pine reached feathery arms upward to the sky, as if pointing the way to consolation and comfort.

Sitting alone in the chilly night air, Zandy hugged her knees and Bible to her chest and prayed. "There must be an answer, Lord. There must be an honorable way out of this. I don't want my family to suffer. I don't want the people to hate me and hurt my brothers. Please help me to know what I must do."

Opening the Bible, Zandy found the words of 1 Thessalonians 4:3. "'For this is the will of God,'" she made out in the bright moonlight, "'even your sanctification, that ye should abstain from fornication.'" It couldn't possibly be any clearer than that. God would not want Zandy to become a mistress even for the noble cause of easing her family's hunger.

"So, if this is Your will, Father," Zandy breathed the prayer, "that I should remain pure and chaste until my marriage, then please show me what I should do to help my family. My father seems determined to discuss this with Riley, and I don't know what will happen then."

Zandy could well imagine Riley's pleasure at her father's demand that she do as Riley wished. Her father would never even know that he was sending his oldest child into a life of sin. Zandy shook her head. The Word was quite clear. The only noble cause was God's cause. She would simply have to work on Riley's heart and win him to God.

But how? Zandy couldn't help but hear her mind ask the question. "How, Lord? How do I get Riley Dawson to act honorably with me and to accept You as his God and Savior?"

Zandy sat on the stoop for hours and, when she finally took herself to bed, it was a fitful sleep that she found waiting for her.

All through the night, Zandy dreamed of Riley Dawson and his smiling, brown-black eyes. She was trying to talk to him, but it was to no avail. Riley would always laugh and go to speak with her father. When Zandy finally woke from the nightmare, it was still dark outside.

She looked down at George and Bart who were snuggled close to each other for warmth. How sweet they were in their innocence! Their faces were so soft and peaceful, lost in their dreams of school and play and better days. How could she not do all in her power to make their lives better?

Zandy finally gave up on sleep and got dressed for the day. She pulled out a dark blue skirt and calico print blouse. Zandy gently fingered the worn lace collar. Once, this blouse had been one of her Sunday best. Now it was used for every day with no hope of a replacement in sight. Riley had said he could give her the finest clothes ever made for a woman to wear. Why should I remember that? Zandy wondered silently. Clothes had never been all that important to her, yet just now it had been the one thing that brought her focus back to Riley.

She dressed quickly and went into the kitchen to stoke the fire. The last of cherry embers were barely warming the cast-iron stove when Zandy put in several pieces of wood and went to the task of preparing breakfast.

Ruth was the next to appear, bringing Molly into the front room in order to feed her. "You're up awfully early, Zandy. I suppose it was difficult to sleep," Ruth said as she put Molly on the floor and went to prepare her a bottle of canned milk.

"Yes," Zandy admitted as she handed Ruth an already warmed bottle.

"Thank you, Zandy," Ruth said as she took the bottle and picked Molly back up. Taking a seat at the kitchen table, Ruth quieted the hungry baby before continuing. "I've never told you this, Zandy, but I feel that it's important."

"What is it, Ruth?" Zandy questioned as she came to sit across from her stepmother.

Ruth looked behind her and then leaned forward, pressing closer to Zandy. "I don't want Burley to overhear me. It might hurt him if he were to hear what I have to say."

Zandy's look of confusion didn't surprise Ruth. She was certain that Zandy would never have expected the words that Ruth was about to share.

"Zandy, when your mother died and left you and your pa, I felt sorry for Burley and, of course, I adored you. I felt it was important to mother you and keep you from losing heart. You were such a fragile, little thing, so sweet and gentle. Yet, there was a streak of stubbornness and independence. I was afraid if someone didn't step in and help, you might go astray and never grow up to be the kind of woman that your ma would have wanted you to be."

Zandy still held the look of confusion. "But what..."

Ruth interrupted her, "Please, let me continue." Ruth repositioned the now sleeping Molly and placed the bottle on the table. "I wasn't in love with your pa," Ruth admitted, and Zandy's confusion changed to surprise. "I think he knew that. But, out of love for him now, I wouldn't want this kind of thing thrown in his face."

"Of course not," Zandy assured. "If you didn't love him, then why did you marry him?"

"I married him because of you. You needed a ma and I already loved you as if you were my own. I'd fallen in love with you the first day you'd come to school with your long dark pigtails and dark green eyes. You were just so precious to me, Zandy, I couldn't risk losing you. Besides, I wasn't getting any younger, and people already called me an old maid. Burley was needy and so was I. The rest just fell into place."

"I see," Zandy said as she leaned her head on her hand.

"I'm not sure you do," Ruth whispered in the dim light. "Zandy, I love Burley with all my heart, but it didn't come overnight. It took years of steady building and working. I just wanted to offer this to you because I know your pa's mind is set on having you accept Riley Dawson's proposal. I thought it might offer you a small bit of comfort to know that many people have been faced with similar problems. Love will come, Zandy. I know you, and Mister Dawson seems kind enough."

Zandy sighed and pushed away from the table. "Riley is a troubled man without a real direction for his life. He is kind enough when he wants to be, yet there is a side of Riley Dawson that frightens me," Zandy admitted and wondered if Ruth would be shocked by her open discussion of Riley.

"Men can be that way," Ruth agreed, "but it usually isn't all that bad. Marriage is work, Zandy. You can't rely on storybooks or fables to base what you think you should be feeling."

"I'm not, Ruth," Zandy said as she poured them both a cup of coffee. "I'm basing it on the Bible. You and Pa have always brought me up to put God first and to stand by the Bible and its truth. But this time, you and Pa both seem to be ignoring some important things in the Word. Please understand, I don't mean any disrespect," Zandy said as she reached the coffee out to her stepmother.

"I know that, Zandy. I don't know why things are the way they are, but I do know that the Bible says to honor your father, and your father wants you to marry Riley Dawson."

"Very well," Zandy said with a heaviness in her heart that she couldn't explain to her stepmother, "If Riley Dawson asks me to marry him, I will say yes."

twelve

Zandy prepared cornmeal mush for breakfast and busied herself by helping the boys to take their places at the table. She couldn't help but consider each bruised face. The only exception was little George who would have gladly bloodied a nose or two himself, had he been bigger.

How she loved her little brothers! She'd always hated being an only child, and when Joshua had been born, Zandy remembered dancing up and down the street telling any neighbor who would listen that she had a new baby brother.

The boys were all abuzz with the details of the fight, and it wasn't until their father joined them at the table that they finally quieted down to eat.

Zandy stood silently in the corner watching the rest of the family as though she weren't even in the room. She listened to her father reprimand the boys for fighting, listened to her stepmother expand on the virtues of being peacemakers, and all the while Zandy knew that it was yet another example of how she was responsible for her family's problems.

After everyone was fed, Zandy took herself up the mountainside to pray and consider her stepmother's words. The day was glorious and the mountainside a riot of color as columbine, daisies, and primroses danced in the wind. Making her way up the path, Zandy barely noticed the world around her. Her mind was still deep in thought from her talk with Ruth.

Zandy would have never imagined in a million years that Ruth and Burley hadn't been perfectly in love when they married. Zandy tried to think back to when Ruth became a part of their family, but nothing in her memories indicated that Ruth hadn't dearly loved her new husband. Zandy sat down on a large rock to think about her fate.

Since they had come to Colorado, nothing had been right. It wasn't that the land wasn't beautiful, but the winters were harsh and so was life in a mining town. Zandy couldn't bear the thought of her father risking his life in the dark, dank hole called a silver mine. Surely, nothing was worth the risk of life that mining created, but as long as people cherished the jingle of gold in their pockets and silver on their table, someone would be willing to risk the lives of others to harvest the precious metal.

Zandy knew it wasn't her imagination that the mining life had aged her family. Both Ruth and Burley had seemed to grow older by the minute and now Zandy knew she was only adding to their burden through her conflict with Riley Dawson.

Her mind went back to the first moment she'd laid eyes on Riley. He was such a strong figure, so self-confident and sure of himself. People always seemed to be drawn to men who had plans of action and weren't afraid to push through for their goals to be accomplished. Riley Dawson was this type of man.

Yet, Zandy couldn't help but think of Riley's honesty the morning after he'd drugged her. He seemed so vulnerable in those moments, and something about his weakness and pain drew Zandy to him almost against her will.

She thought of the young man he must have been and couldn't help but wonder what his life might have been like if he'd remained with his parents instead of going to college in the east. She reminded herself that most likely he would have been killed with his parents and, for some reason that bothered her a great deal.

Absentmindedly, Zandy was reaching down and picking a flower when the peacefulness of her day was disturbed.

"I saw you walking up here." It was Jim Williams. "I just wanted to have a word with you before I left Dawson."

"You're leaving?" Zandy questioned in surprise.

"That's right, not that I expect you or anyone else to care," Jim said as he pushed back his hat.

"Why do you say that? Of course we'll care," Zandy said as she eyed Jim carefully. Something about his manner seemed strained.

"Don't play games with me, Zandy. I know all about you and Dawson," Jim said bitterly.

"Don't tell me that you've been given over to believing gossip."

"It isn't gossip that you spent the night at the Dawson mansion. I saw you leave the house."

"I see," Zandy said as she discarded the flower and got to her feet. She smoothed her dark blue skirt and straightened up.

"That's all you have to say for yourself? If I'd known you were a fast woman, I'd have never wasted a moment of time on you. I think you've deceived a great many people, including Riley Dawson."

"Why do you say that?" Zandy questioned. She was growing steadily more angry as Jim hurled his accusations.

"Well," Jim began, "the way I see it he wanted to marry you because he thought you were honorable. But now he knows better. Doesn't he?"

Zandy wanted to slap him, but she refrained from even stepping a single inch closer. "You're no different than the others," Zandy said angrily. "I did nothing wrong! I collapsed at the Dawson mansion, nothing more, nothing less. My father had just been blown up, my stepmother was gravely ill, and I hadn't had a decent meal in weeks. I fainted, Jim. Does that disappoint you?" Zandy hated lying but she wasn't about to incriminate Riley in any wrongdoings. That would only make it sound like she was making up stories to defend her position.

For several minutes, Jim said nothing. Then, with a shrug of his shoulders, he turned to leave. "It doesn't matter. Everybody already believes they know what happened."

"Yes, Jim, and just how is it that everyone learned that I'd spent the night at the Dawson mansion? You didn't by any chance have anything to do with the spreading of that story, did you?"

Jim again shrugged his shoulders. "I don't see that it

much matters how everyone found out."

"Look, Jim," Zandy said as she sat back down on the rock. "I tried to be a friend to you and also to Riley. I tried to be kind and honest with everyone. I simply don't care what you or anybody else thinks. So please, just leave me alone." Zandy delivered the words firmly with emphasis on the word "alone." That word seemed to sum up her life more than any other. She was alone, with the exception of her Heavenly Father.

Jim opened his mouth to say something and then apparently thought better of it.

Zandy watched him retreat down the mountainside and put her head in her hands to cry. She'd never been given to tears, but this was too much.

"Why, Lord," she sobbed into her hands. "Why has everyone turned against me?"

Riley Dawson watched Jim Williams as he disappeared down the mountain. Having seen Zandy go up the mountain, with Jim close behind, Riley hadn't known what to expect when he followed them, but the confrontation between Zandy and his former employee wasn't at all what he'd anticipated.

So, Jim was responsible for letting people believe that Alexandra had spent the night with me, Riley thought to himself. If Williams hadn't already quit his job, Riley would have fired him. Why did it suddenly seem so important to defend Alexandra's honor?

Riley moved from where he'd been hiding. Zandy's sobs tore at his heart, and yet they caused Riley to feel very cautious. Not knowing what to do, Riley depended upon his arrogance to shield him from feeling too much.

"I see you're finally alone," Riley said as he approached Zandy.

Zandy dried her eyes on the back of her sleeve and got to her feet. "What are you doing here?" she questioned, trying to compose her voice.

"I saw Mister Williams make his way up the path after you and thought you might need my help."

Zandy started to laugh until big tears streamed down her face. She was very near to hysteria from the tension and pressure when Riley took hold of her arms and shook her firmly.

"Stop it, Alexandra. Stop it now," Riley said, the concern clearly evident in his voice.

Zandy tried to compose herself. She looked Riley square in the face and tried to shake off his hold. "Let go of me!"

"As you wish," Riley said and dropped his hands. "Why didn't you tell Jim the truth?"

"I don't know what you mean."

"You told him you fainted at my house. Why didn't you tell him that I drugged you?"

Zandy shrugged. "What would it have gained me? If I'd told people about the coffee, who would've believed me? Who would have cared about the truth when the lies were so much easier to believe?"

"And you've never told your folks that I wanted you as a mistress and not as a wife. Why?"

"I was afraid to," Zandy admitted. "I was afraid my father would defend my honor and lose his job or worse. The one thing I didn't count on was my parents' giving up on me."

"But now that Mister Williams has given up on you as well as your folks, I guess you have nowhere else to turn."

"That's not true," Zandy said, trying to defend herself. "I'll always have God."

The wind blew across the mountainside, and with it the rich scent of honeysuckle and pine filled the air. Riley reached out to touch Zandy's cheek. Zandy was too tired to care and allowed him to stroke her face. "You're at the end of the road, Zandy. You have to make a choice."

"I thought I had," Zandy said softly as she lifted her green eyes to meet Riley's intense stare. Her heart beat faster, and she could feel her hands trembling.

Neither one said anything for several minutes. The world seemed suspended in time, and even the rippling mountain streams and quaking aspen were muted in the silence of Zandy's mind.

"What do your folks think about all of this?" Riley finally questioned as he took a step backward.

"They want me to marry you," Zandy answered honestly. "I promised my stepmother that if you asked me to marry you, I would say yes."

Riley looked stunned. "You what?"

Zandy leaned back against the rock. "I told Ruth that I would marry you."

"Is that true?" Riley questioned. "I mean, knowing everything that I've done to you and what I've tried to make you do."

"Yes," Zandy whispered. "In order to save my family and help the town out, I would marry you, Riley."

Riley seemed so taken aback by Zandy's declaration that he had to sit down. Zandy continued to watch him, but said nothing.

"Why?" Riley questioned hoarsely.

"Why?" Zandy asked in surprise. "Why do you suppose?"

"I'm not really sure," Riley replied.

Zandy was surprised at the turn the conversation had taken. Always before Riley Dawson had seemingly had the upper hand in their relationship. Sensing a softening in his attitude, Zandy forced an issue that had long been on her mind.

"Why do I have to be your mistress, Riley? I will never have a willing heart to do such a thing," she said. "I will, however, offer a compromise and marry you."

"You're being completely honest with me? You would marry me?"

"Yes."

Riley ran his hand back through his hair. "All right, Alexandra Stewart. I accept your compromise."

"When?" Zandy asked, trying not to show her surprise. She hadn't expected Riley to agree to marriage.

"What do you suggest?"

"I guess the sooner the better. I don't think the children can hold out much longer," Zandy answered as she got to her feet.

"Tomorrow, then?"

"All right, Riley. Will you make the arrangements?"

"Yes," he answered softly. "Is there anything I can get you to help you ready yourself?"

"No, nothing for myself," Zandy answered as she

looked at her husband-to-be, "but if you would send some food to my family, I would be most appreciative."

"Of course," Riley said and watched Zandy resolve herself to the arrangement. Why didn't he feel victorious in the matter? He'd gotten his way—at least in a matter of speaking. As he watched Zandy walk slowly down the pathway, Riley felt a wave of guilt wash over him. Would he really be able to go through with the wedding?

thirteen

Zandy stared at her reflection in the mirror. The woman who stared back didn't seem to be the same one who looked into the glass. Ruth had helped Zandy pile her long brown hair on top of her head and arranged it into an attractive bun. Next, they took the wisps that fell down around Zandy's face and used hot irons to curl them into framing tendrils.

Zandy's dress was the same one Ruth had worn when she had married Burley. It was a lovely gown created out of a pale blue sateen. The sleeves were long and trimmed in handmade lace, and the bodice was high to the neck with pleated folds and dark blue trim. The dress had been designed for a fashionable cage bustle, but having no such luxury at hand, Zandy and Ruth had compensated by using layers of rolled dish towels pinned to Zandy's petticoat. The final touch was Ruth's only remaining pair of kid leather boots which, although a tiny bit large for Zandy, were more than adequate for the purpose of getting married in.

The boys had gone out to collect flowers for Zandy's bouquet and Burley, determined to attend his daughter's marriage to Riley Dawson, had freshly blackened his boots. The entire Stewart household was busy with the details of the upcoming ceremony. No one seemed to pay any attention to the fact that the bride was less than festive in her preparations.

Riley sent word that the wedding would take place at two o'clock in the newly reopened church. Zandy acknowledged the news with nothing more than a nod of her head, and Ruth returned the message bearer with the Stewart family's approval.

Now with less than twenty minutes until the two o'clock deadline, Zandy couldn't help but feel uneasy about having given her approval to marry Riley. Love will come, Ruth had told her, but Zandy couldn't help but wonder if it were possible to hope for such a thing under the circumstances.

The boys burst through the doorway with handfuls of mountain flowers, each proudly bearing his contribution to Zandy's wedding bouquet. They adored their big sister and, while they didn't relish the idea of Zandy's going to live in the house on the hill, each one had enjoyed the food that Riley had sent the night before. Riley had even seen to it that a small bakery cake had been included, and the boys thought this extraordinary.

"Are you ready?" Ruth questioned Zandy as she came into the room.

"I guess so," Zandy answered, looking about her as if there were something she was forgetting.

"Did you get your things packed?" Ruth asked softly.

"Yes," Zandy replied in a hollow voice. "I'll have somebody come get them later," she added.

"Zandy, please don't hate us for insisting on this marriage. You know we just love you, and we want good things for you. Riley Dawson can give you good things, and he cares deeply for you."

"Do you really think so?" Zandy surprised them both by voicing the question.

"How can you ask that? He wants to marry you, and just look at the lengths he's gone to in order to get you to say yes."

Zandy's puzzled look mirrored the questions in her heart. How could everyone be so forgiving of Riley's deeds just because they thought he was a man in love? If only they knew the truth, Zandy thought to herself. How admirable would Riley Dawson be then?

Ruth pretended not to notice her stepdaughter's less than jubilant spirit. She comforted herself with the assurance that it was a case of bridal nerves, and nothing more but the look on Zandy's face made Ruth wonder for a fleeting moment if they were doing the right thing.

"You should see all the people!" Bart exclaimed at the top of his voice. "The whole town is coming to see you get married, Zandy."

Zandy turned, horror stricken, to Ruth. "He didn't invite the whole town, did he?"

"Now, Zandy," Ruth said with a gentle pat to her stepdaughter's arm, "he's just proud to be marrying you. Let him show off if he wants."

Zandy felt her knees give way, and Ruth quickly pulled her to a chair. "I'm not sure that I can go through with this," Zandy whispered, but Ruth didn't hear her.

"What was that?" Ruth asked as she brought a cold cloth to Zandy.

"Nothing," Zandy murmured. There was no sense in backing out now. Everyone was too happy, too pleased, in fact, that the honorable Mister Dawson was to be happily married to the bride of his choosing.

How can I face him and not faint? Zandy wondered to herself. The cold cloth did little to settle her dizziness. She knew how he'd be, all smug and self-assured. No one, including Riley Dawson, would care how she felt. And how did she feel? More than once Zandy had asked herself this very question.

A part of her was relieved to know that her family would be provided for and she herself could go into an honorable arrangement. Yet, in the back of her mind, was the knowledge that Riley wasn't saved and he didn't appear inclined to be saved in the near future.

How could she walk down the aisle of the church, participating in a ceremony she'd dreamed of since being a little child, and know what a mockery she was making of the values and principles she'd been taught to follow all of her life?

"It's time to go," Ruth interrupted Zandy's fearful thoughts.

Zandy felt a wave of panic, and it was all she could do to follow her stepmother out the door and down the pathway to the church.

Beautiful music was coming from the church. So many people had gathered that they were now standing outside the building, just to catch a glimpse of Riley Dawson's bride. The "Oohs" and "Ahhs" went unnoticed by Zandy whose troubled heart was consuming her every thought. It was much like a lamb being led to the slaughter.

The same thought occurred to Riley who stood resplendent in his elegantly tailored suit at the front of the church. Zandy wouldn't allow herself to even look at him, fearful that she'd bolt and run, further disgracing her family.

Riley knew that she was purposefully avoiding his eyes, and the thought only troubled him more. A young woman should desire to gaze lovingly into the eyes of the man she was about to join herself to for life. But, Riley concluded, this young woman didn't love him, nor did she want to be joined to him for life.

Burley led his daughter to her place beside her husband-to-be and, when he handed Zandy to Riley, he ignored the trembling in his daughter's hand. Riley, however, couldn't ignore it, knowing that it was caused by fear and not innocent anticipation.

Zandy tried her best to control her emotions. She squeezed back tears more than once and took deep breaths just to get through the ceremony without fainting. She heard her name being read as if it belonged to someone else and thought the same of the voice that agreed to honor and obey the man who now gripped her arm.

She swayed only once, when Riley promised himself to her until death, and felt a small amount of relief when Riley most capably steadied her so that no one else would know of her weakening. But Riley knew, and that troubled Zandy most deeply. She had no desire to appear delicate and frail in his eyes. She bolstered her courage, and when Pastor Brokamp announced that they were man and wife, Zandy boldly lifted her face to receive her husband's kiss. Her eyes, however, remained closed.

Riley placed a brief, gentle kiss upon his bride's lips then turned her to face the applause and shouts of approval from the congregation.

"Please, get me out of here, Riley," she managed to whisper against his ear. The display looked as if she were murmuring some endearment to her new husband, causing the crowds to respond even louder.

Riley looked down at the paleness of Zandy's face and knew that she wouldn't last much longer. For once in his life, he was feeling quite responsible for his actions and didn't care for the way it made him feel.

"If I can have everyone's attention," Riley shouted above the crowd. "There are to be refreshments in the town hall and a dance in the park this evening." More cheers rose up, and Zandy felt herself grip Riley's arm tightly to steady her weakening knees. "We will, of course, join you later. There are picture sittings to take care of and such, so do feel free to go ahead and enjoy yourselves."

Riley pulled Zandy along through the crowd of well-wishers. She could hardly make her legs move and yet, because of Riley's persistance, found herself out on the church lawn being positioned for her wedding picture.

"Now, Mrs. Dawson, if you'll just put your hand on your husband's shoulder, like this," the photographer was saying, and Zandy found herself faced with the stunning revelation that she was no longer Zandy Stewart but Alexandra Dawson.

She posed mechanically, waiting in rigid position as the camera was readied. Burley and Ruth stood looking on, while the boys ran circles around the entire group.

When the photographer announced that he was finished, Zandy breathed a sigh of relief. Now, perhaps she could retreat to the sanctuary of home, but where was home?

Without realizing what was happening, Zandy found herself being embraced by a teary-eyed Ruth. She was saying something to Zandy about the wedding but, for the life of her, Zandy couldn't concentrate on the words. Then Burley was telling her how proud he was of her sacrifice and how he wouldn't forget her generosity to her family.

Zandy gazed beyond her parents to her brothers who were now being beckoned to come say goodbye to their big sister.

"But I don't want Zandy to go away," George began to cry. He was only coming to understand that Zandy's wedding meant she'd now be taking up residence elsewhere. Up until that moment, the wedding had been nothing more than a big party to him.

As George began to wail and grip Zandy tightly, Zandy couldn't help but cry, too. She picked up George and held him close to her, both crying over the inevitable separation. Riley grew uncomfortable and made the excuse of needing to see the photographer before he got away. Ruth and Burley tried to soothe their children, but to no avail.

Soon, Samuel began to whimper, too, and then it was only a matter of time before Bart joined in. Joshua stood staunchly grown up, trying to appear a responsible example for his brothers, but tears formed in his eyes as well.

Finally, Burley put an end to the misery, forcing George away from Zandy. Zandy could see that the action caused her father a great deal of pain and tried to calm George as Burley pulled him away.

"Now, George, you know you can come see me whenever you want," Zandy said as she took a handkerchief from Ruth and dried her tears. "All of you can come see me."

"Of course, they can," Riley reaffirmed as he joined Zandy and her family. "You're all welcome in our home any time."

"Thank you, Mister Dawson," Burley said as he placed George on the ground. The pain of his actions showed clearly in his face.

"I think we should be on a first name basis. After all," Riley stated, "we're family."

"That's true," Burley agreed. "I hadn't thought much about it, but you're right."

Ruth was already herding her little family up the path toward home so, after giving Zandy a quick peck on the cheek, Burley excused himself and hurried after his family.

Zandy watched them until they were nearly home. A part of her heart went with them...a part of her that Riley could never have, no matter what.

After having made their rounds to the various festivities, Riley led an exhausted and thoroughly spent Zandy home. Neither one spoke as they walked the path to the mansion. The evening was warm and the night sky was a rich ebony with stars so brilliant and close that they looked as if you could reach up and touch them.

Scents of honeysuckle and rose assaulted Zandy's nose as they passed through the Dawson gardens and on into the house. Riley ushered Zandy into the library and called for Mrs. Malloy to bring her something cold to drink.

Mrs. Malloy arrived with a cold pitcher of lemonade, praising the freighters for the shipment of lemons that made the drink possible. Seeing that neither Riley nor Zandy were in a mood to talk, Mrs. Malloy made her way out of the room as quickly as she'd arrived.

Riley considered his silent wife as he offered her a glass of lemonade. He'd been unable to shake the feeling of guilt that had assaulted him from the first moment he'd agreed to marry her. It was clear to him that she'd not come willingly into this marriage, and his pride sorely pricked his conscience, reminding him of his desire for her willingness.

Unable to bear the silence any longer, Riley got to his feet. "I'm sorry to do this, but I must leave for a time. It seems that one of my investments is having severe financial difficulties, and the matter requires my immediate attention."

Zandy looked up in surprise and nearly dropped her glass. "You're leaving?"

"Yes," Riley said in a rather disinterested way. He felt the desperate need to distance himself from his new wife.

"When will you be back?" Zandy questioned.

"I'm not entirely sure, but don't worry. If you need anything at all, clothes, food, whatever, just ask Mrs.

Malloy to send for it. Or, if you prefer, feel free to go shopping. You'll have an unlimited line of credit at any of the establishments."

Zandy's mouth dropped open. "Unlimited?"

Riley's hard look softened. "I tried to tell you I'd take good care of you. I'm a very generous man, Alexandra."

"What about my family?" Zandy couldn't help but dare the question.

"They've already been taken care of. I made you a promise, and I always keep my promises," Riley stated firmly as he moved toward the door. "Now, I need to pack a few things. Do as you like with the house. Choose any bedroom you want, decorate, order new furniture, whatever your heart desires."

Before Zandy could reply, Riley was gone. She sank back wearily against the brocade sofa and studied the room. Books lined the walls to the ceiling, oak shelves and a massive fireplace of limestone and native rock demanded the entire west wall.

Looking farther, Zandy was more than aware of the fine, delicate figurines that had been carefully placed to complement the furnishings of the room. Rich tapestries and ornately framed paintings hung above her head, and expensive furniture from another time and place adorned nearly every corner of the room.

Never in her life had Zandy felt so out of place. Hearing Riley's heavy steps on the staircase, Zandy was surprised when his muted "Goodbye" filtered through the huge double doors. Only one question came to her mind as she heard her husband leave the house. "What have I done?"

Riley made his way to the small cottage behind the mansion. With bag in hand, he came bounding through the door, surprising K.C. Russell. K.C. eyed him curiously, but never voiced the question on his mind.

"I don't want anyone to know I'm staying here," Riley said as he tossed his bag into one of the rooms. "Do you understand?"

"Sure, boss," K.C. said, the surprise still reflected in his stare.

"I'll take Jim's old room," Riley said as he followed his bag into the empty bedroom. Slamming the door behind him, Riley felt ready to pull out his hair. Instead, he flung himself down in the only available chair and wondered aloud, "What have I done?"

fourteen

After a week of seeing no one, save the house staff, Zandy decided to go see her family. She contemplated her new lifestyle as she walked the narrow dirt pathway to her former home. How strange it was to suddenly be married and living in a place that seemed foreign to her. Stranger still was to be a bride without a husband.

"Lord," Zandy found herself praying as she walked, "I still believe in Your promises and I still desire to seek Your will above my own. Protect me from the evil in this world and keep my heart ever thirsty for You."

The crispness of the morning air betrayed the fact that autumn would soon be upon them. There were other signs as well. The aspen trees were already beginning to show signs of changing color, creeping vines that had once been dark green were now decorating the hillsides in ribbons of scarlet and amber, and the sunlight was filtered and diffused as the daylight hours became shorter and shorter.

Zandy sighed and wondered silently what the winter hours of confinement would bring. Could she really bear to wander around the big house all alone? Even a baby of her own would be something to look forward to, but there wasn't even a possibility of that. She found her cheeks growing hot at the thought of having Riley's baby. She couldn't help but wonder what the town of Dawson might think if they knew that she and Riley had never lived together as man and wife.

The Stewart shanty was strangely quiet as Zandy approached the door. She knocked, but when no one answered, she opened the door and walked in. To her shock and surprise, the house was empty.

A search of each room revealed the same thing as the one before it. All personal effects had been stripped away and, while some of the cruder furniture remained, there was no other sign that human life had even dwelt within the walls.

Zandy rushed out the door and made her way into town. She hurried to the jailhouse, thinking that perhaps one of Riley's men would know where her family had gone.

Pat Folkes met her at the door. "Mornin', Missus Dawson. What can I do for you?"

"My family has moved," she stated matter-of-factly. "I was hoping you might tell me where they've gone."

"Sure," Pat said as he took a seat behind a worn desk. "I figured Riley would've told you. He had us move them to the old Mulvane house. You know where that is, don't you?"

Zandy nodded. The Mulvane house was one of the best houses in town. Only Riley's mansion could outshine it as far as size and grace. "How long have they been there?" Zandy questioned.

"We moved them in the day after your wedding."

Zandy was so surprised that she said nothing more as she left the jail and made her way to the Mulvane house.

Long before she reached the stone-step entryway of the Mulvane house, Zandy was hailed by her brothers.

"Zandy! Look, it's Zandy!" Bart called out.

The other boys dropped what they were playing with and hurried down the walkway to greet their sister. George fairly wrapped himself around his older sister's frame.

"Zandy, are you coming back to live with us?" George asked innocently.

Silently Zandy wished that she were, but instead she shook her head. "No, silly, I've just come to make sure that you're still washing behind your ears."

At this George unwound himself from Zandy and backed off. "I forgot."

"Just as I suspected," Zandy said in a teasing voice. "Where's Mama and Molly?"

"They're in the house," Joshua began. "You should see the house, Zandy! It's bigger than our house back in Missouri and loads nicer."

"There's even a lamp hanging down from the ceiling in the front room," George said, notably impressed by their new chandelier.

"I see," Zandy said as she lovingly patted each of her brothers on the head.

"Zandy!" Ruth exclaimed from the doorway. "Come on in. I've missed you so much."

Zandy made her way into the house and allowed Ruth to lead the way from room to room. All the while she explained how Riley had provided them with every convenience and had even given Burley a desk job in the mining office.

When Zandy left some hours later, she felt happy to see her family doing so well and yet was troubled because she knew they could've had comfort much sooner had she not been so disagreeable.

Resolving to show Riley her gratitude, Zandy decided to do whatever it took to become a good wife. She thought of her behavior the day of her wedding and knew that Riley must have been put off by her self-suffering mood.

"Father," Zandy prayed, "I realize that I've not treated Riley very kindly. I realize people change and that they need to be forgiven and, just like all Your other children, I'm in need of forgiving, too. I'm asking You to forgive me for the way I've acted, and to help me to be a good wife to Riley. I know that You can work miracles, so please help me to love him as one of Your creations and to be a good example of Christ's love so that he might accept Jesus as his Savior, Amen."

Zandy felt as if a weight had been lifted from her shoulders. She hurried to the mansion that'd become her home and set about making a list of things she needed or thought would be appreciated by her husband.

When yet another week had passed and Saturday morning dawned bright and cold, Zandy was beginning to worry about Riley and where he might be. When she heard voices in the hallway below, she hurried down the grand staircase to see if it was her husband.

Disappointment lined her expression as she realized it was just Mrs. Malloy directing one of the staff to take upstairs some of the things Zandy had ordered from town.

Zandy led the way back to her bedroom's sitting room and instructed the man to leave everything on the large oval table that occupied the center of the room. After he'd departed, Zandy began to open the boxes to inspect the contents.

Most of the boxes contained clothes as Zandy had felt she had nothing to wear worthy of her status as Riley's wife. She had the town's seamstress working overtime to create several new gowns for immediate delivery while leaving a more extensive order for those that could come later.

Zandy opened a large dress box to reveal a dark green velvet gown that had been lavishly trimmed in black velvet ribbon and lace. She couldn't suppress a gasp of pleasure as she pulled it up to her body and whirled around the room.

"You look charming. Like a little girl in a candy store," Riley spoke from the open door of Zandy's sitting room.

"Riley!" Zandy couldn't help but exclaim. "I was beginning to think you were never coming home."

"I'm not here for long," Riley said as he crossed the room to where Zandy stood holding the dress. It was all he could do to keep from pulling her into his arms.

Zandy felt her knees begin to tremble at the closeness of her husband. She swallowed hard and tried to sound calm. "Oh, I see," she replied softly, and Riley couldn't help but wonder if it was disappointment in her voice or his imagination.

"I see you've gone shopping," Riley went on.

"Yes. I thought it might be necessary to make myself more presentable to the public. I mean," she paused and blushed crimson, "now that I'm your wife."

"I think that's wise. Have you ordered anything else?" he asked, and Zandy felt certain that he was genuinely interested.

"More clothes," Zandy laughed. "I'm afraid I came to you with nothing much more than the clothes on my back. Now, how about you? Where have you been all this time? I thought you might have at least come back to the house once or twice during the last two weeks."

"My, my," Riley teased, "don't you sound the part of the nagging housewife."

Zandy shrugged her shoulders. "It's just common courtesy. I couldn't tell anyone where you'd gone. I mean if someone would have needed you."

"I told my men," Riley said as he reached out and fingered one of the black velvet ribbons.

"Oh," Zandy said, rather disappointed that Riley would confide in his men and not in her.

"This dress is lovely. The color matches your eyes," Riley said softly. "Would you like to wear it to the dance tonight?"

"What dance? Where is it?" Zandy questioned a bit more excitedly than she'd intended.

Riley laughed. "It's a celebration dance. We've just opened another silver mine. I've called it the Alexandra Mine."

"After me?"

"Who else?" Riley said with a smile. "It only seemed fitting that I should. Now, do you want to go with me or not?"

"Are you sure you can give me the time?" Zandy asked in mock sarcasm.

Riley pulled Zandy into his arms, crushing the velvet gown between them. "I have more than time to give you, Alexandra." He lowered his lips to hers in a hungry kiss that betrayed his desire. Just as quickly he let Zandy go and stepped back abruptly. "Sorry, I got carried away."

Zandy frowned in confusion. "You are my husband." The words were out before Zandy had even realized she was speaking.

Riley said nothing, but the lightheartedness of the moment was clearly broken.

Zandy thought quickly of some way to take Riley's mind off of her words. "I wanted to thank you for all you've done for my family. I went to see them last week, and they're all so happy, Riley. I know it was my fault that I let things go on for so long. . . ." Zandy's words trailed into silence as she moved away from Riley's quizzical stare.

She was moving in painstaking slowness to place the velvet gown on a hanger, hoping the extra time would allow her to regain her composure. It was difficult to explain to Riley that she was still uncertain that she'd done the right thing in marrying him, but now that it was done she did want to honor him and be a good wife in the eyes of God.

"I'm glad you're pleased with my arrangements for your family," Riley said as he came up behind her.

Zandy could feel his breath upon her neck and silently wished that she hadn't pinned her hair up. At least if it were down, she reasoned, she wouldn't feel his presence so keenly.

Zandy said nothing and, having placed the dress in the wardrobe, she had no other alternative but to turn and face Riley. When she did, she felt her breath catch in her throat. She was attracted to him, she knew that was beyond denying. There was something in his dark hair and eyes that seemed to draw in her heart and mind. She briefly contemplated thoughts of his forcing her into marriage and suddenly wasn't sure that she cared anymore.

Riley reached out his hand to touch her face. His fingers were light upon her cheek, causing Zandy to tremble. "Now, what about the dance? Will you accompany me?"

"Of course," Zandy whispered.

"Remember, you have to dance with the one who brings you," Riley's eyes twinkled in amusement, but Zandy knew he was also quite serious.

"I would love to dance with you, Mr. Dawson," she answered boldly.

Riley's ear-to-ear grin betrayed his pleasure with her answer. "That's good, Mrs. Dawson," he said with emphasis on her married name, "because I intend to dance your slippers off."

"I accept your challenge with pleasure," Zandy said with a smile. It had been a long time since she'd danced and an even longer time since she'd felt this happy.

Zandy had never danced so much in her life. Now that she was Mrs. Riley Dawson, she was most eagerly sought out and graciously respected. Zandy, in turn, was guardedly kind and received each compliment with cautious hospitality.

As she found herself dancing with one of the store owners who had formerly turned her away from his door, Zandy was amused at the way the man seemed to gush in conversation of the well-stocked shelves and complete inventory of his mercantile. He ended the dance by telling Zandy that he'd be most honored if she would remember him when she needed store goods.

At that comment, Zandy rolled her eyes back. She was surprised, however, to find Riley's laughing eyes fixed firmly on her expression, and she quickly lowered her face, flushed in embarrassment.

"I believe this dance is mine," Riley said as he came forward to claim his wife.

"You know what they say about dancing too many dances with one person," Zandy teased. "People will believe you're quite gone on me."

Riley leaned his face closer to Zandy's. "And they would be right," he whispered against her ear.

Riley's warm breath on her neck made Zandy quiver. She wondered if Riley was telling the truth or merely making small talk.

When the dance ended, Riley suggested some refreshments. "After all," he said in an amused tone, "I paid for them."

He had just handed Zandy a glass of punch when a loud explosion rocked the ground.

Riley looked down at his watch. "Um," he said as he noted the time. "It's already ten-thirty. Sounds like the boys must have blown quite a bit of face rock tonight."

Zandy nodded. She knew very well that each shift ended their work hours by blasting out new ore. It would then be the responsibility of the in-coming shift to pick up the rock and send the ore on for processing.

The musicians were now taking a break, and Riley suggested that he and Zandy take a walk. Zandy was grateful to escape the stares and whispers of the others.

She laughed to herself when one woman had told her that married life obviously agreed with her.

Riley and Zandy had barely taken a step out the door when they were greeted by the loud ominous sound of the mine's whistle. The five short blasts followed by a long one was the signal that everyone dreaded to hear—FIRE!

Riley pulled Zandy aside as the crowd of dancers came rushing out to take up the cause of fighting the fire in their evening finery.

Zandy started out after them, but Riley pulled her back. "Where do you think you're going?"

"We have to help," Zandy insisted.

"I'll go help, but I don't want you in danger," Riley stated firmly.

"I can't just sit by and wonder what has happened. There are injured people down there. I might be no good at fighting the fire, but I can help with the nursing duties."

Riley's expression betrayed his concern. He studied Zandy's determined face and agreed. "Let's go. But you stay away from the mine itself."

Zandy nodded and hiked up her skirt to race after her long-legged husband.

The chaos at the mine was quickly organized. Miners who hadn't been injured in the explosion were busy carrying buckets of water from Corner Creek, and a line of people had been formed to pass the buckets down.

Zandy quickly learned that six men had been killed and another dozen injured when one of the Burleigh drills had exploded causing a chain reaction that ignited a nearby case of dynamite. She went to work, mindless of the new green velvet gown, washing off wounds, applying tourniquets, and helping the company doctor to organize his patients. At one point when the doctor was anxiously awaiting delivery of bandaging materials, Zandy pulled off her petticoat and began to tear it into strips.

The doctor nodded approvingly and smiled. He admired the young woman's ingenuity and disregard for her own material possessions.

Zandy recognized many of the men who'd been hurt and tried to comfort them and later their families, as the night progressed into the wee hours of morning.

Finally, at four-thirty, the fire had been extinguished, and the wounded had been cared for as best they could. Litters were brought to carry the injured to a makeshift hospital in one of the empty buildings on the Dawson estate.

Zandy had directed Riley's men, K.C. and Pat, to lead the way and make every necessary effort to aid the doctor.

Riley had stood to one side contemplating his young wife's ability to organize the tragedy. He offered no interference when Zandy sent Mike Muldair down to Edwards' General Store with orders to bring back the supplies they needed.

When everything had calmed to a reasonable level of order, Riley took hold of Zandy's arm and motioned for her that it was time to leave.

"Come on, we've done all we can. Better get some rest. There'll be plenty to do tomorrow, or I guess I should say, later today," Riley declared.

"I suppose you're right. I hate to leave them, though. I know what it is to worry and fret over your injured loved ones," Zandy said as she allowed Riley to lead her home. "I'll never forget the feeling when they brought my father home."

"You were quite hysterical, as I recall," Riley interjected.

"I was beyond rational thought," Zandy admitted, "or I'd have never come crawling to you." The words were out before she'd thought of how they might be received. Her hand flew quickly to her mouth and her eyes flew open. The regret was clearly stated in her eyes.

"It's all right, Zandy," Riley said as he tucked her arm close against his body and patted her hand. "I deserved that."

"But I didn't mean. . .I mean we're married now and . . .," Zandy fell silent, trying desperately to figure her way out of the situation.

Riley stopped and gently pulled her into his arms. Zandy said nothing, mesmerized by the tenderness she found in Riley's eyes. "Forcing you to marry me didn't really change anything, Alexandra. I'm just starting to figure that out."

Zandy could feel her heart pounding. She was more than just a little aware of Riley's strong, well-muscled body and deeply embarrassed in her innocence.

Riley reached up to wipe a bit of soot from Zandy's cheek, and the touch was electrifying. Zandy shuddered at the touch, and Riley misread it for revulsion. He frowned slightly, wishing that he could make things better.

"I'm sorry," he said as he dropped his arms.

Zandy's expression of wonderment changed instantly to one of confusion. "What?" her one-word question kept Riley from walking away from her.

"I know things aren't right," Riley said as he pulled Zandy with him toward the house. In his mind he was still seeing the faces of the dead men. Men whose lives had been snuffed out in a flash of explosives and fire. One minute they'd been living, breathing beings with families and homes. The next, they were just objects of grief and pain.

Zandy waited for Riley to open the door, but he didn't. She looked at the strange expression on his face, wondering desperately what he could be thinking.

"I'd better say good night. I need to think, and I can't do it here," Riley suddenly said. "I won't be back for a while, so don't wait up for me."

Zandy watched him walk away. He seemed to have aged twenty years in a few short moments. What had she done to cause his pain, and where was he going at this hour? The only place open would be the saloon.

The thought of Riley's drinking his troubles away grieved Zandy. She'd never thought about it before, but perhaps that's where Riley had been spending all his time.

Angrily, Zandy stormed into the house, slamming the door behind her. "Good riddance," she said aloud. For a few brief minutes she'd almost allowed herself to believe that Riley cared.

fifteen

Riley sat in the darkness of the mining office. It was Sunday morning so there wouldn't be anyone coming to disturb him. Yet it wasn't outside influences that were disturbing his peace of mind—the conflict was coming from within.

He couldn't forget the faces of the dead miners. He couldn't close out the picture of the wives as they held their dead husbands and cried. Life was not the enduring, lasting thing he'd thought it to be. It was in fact, quite fragile and short.

Riley couldn't help but think of the times Zandy had tried to share God's way with him. He'd ignored her just as he had his parents. But that was when he'd felt immortal.

Putting his head in his hands, Riley knew that his life was a mess. He lived on the whim of the silver market, not even needing to put his hand to any real work. He'd forced a beautiful, vital woman into marriage knowing full well that she hated him. No, Riley thought to himself, Zandy could never hate anyone.

He thought of Zandy's gentle spirit and enduring nature. She'd put up the best fight he'd ever known, and all to maintain her values and faith. He'd never known anyone who'd held their conviction so solidly when adversity threatened to destroy all that they loved.

Thinking of Zandy caused Riley more grief than he

wanted to deal with. He couldn't shame her by divorcing her, but neither could he bring himself to shame her by expecting her to be a real wife to him. She didn't have a willing heart and, from the way she seemed repulsed by his touch, Riley didn't expect her to have one any time soon.

As sunlight filtered in through the drawn shades, peace continued to elude Riley Dawson. Determined to ignore his fears and mortality, Riley put his head down on the desk and went to sleep.

Riley slept and, as he did, he dreamed of being at home with his mother and father. His mother was reminding him of Psalm Twenty-three's promise.

He could hear her tell him in her sweet, loving voice, "Remember, Riley, when you belong to God there is nothing the world can do to you that will best what God has planned. 'The Lord is my shepherd; I shall not want.' He will never allow you to want for anything, so long as you lie down beside Him."

"Mama," Riley whispered in his sleep. He felt his mind being forced into consciousness, but he wanted so much to stay in the dream with his mother.

"Don't forget, 'Yea, though I walk through the valley of the shadow of death, I will fear no evil: for thou art with me. . .,'" his mother's voice faded with those words.

Riley sat up with a start. Thinking of the Psalm, he rubbed the sleep from his eyes and got up. "Fear no evil?" he said aloud with a laugh. "But everyone thinks I am evil, and how can I not fear myself knowing exactly who I am and what I've done?"

Riley opened the door of the mining office and was

surprised to find the sun already starting to set. He'd had
no idea that he'd slept so long. Pushing back the
thoughts that troubled him most, Riley made his way up
the hillside.

When Riley appeared at breakfast the following morning, Zandy couldn't suppress her surprise.

"What are you doing here?" she asked as she swished
across the dining room dressed smartly in a pink-and-
white-striped day dress.

Riley lifted his eyes from his coffee cup and smiled.
"I thought you might enjoy an outing. I know I've not
been good company, and I want to make it up to you."

"I see," Zandy answered in a guarded tone. She sat
down at the table and accepted a platter of food from
Mrs. Malloy.

"You look very nice," Riley offered in a way of
conversation.

"Thank you," Zandy said with a blush. She still found
it difficult to accept compliments from Riley. "What
kind of outing do you have in mind?"

"I wanted to show you where the Alexandra Mine is.
It's not yet working full time, and today it's closed in
honor of the dead. Still, I'd like to show you your
namesake."

Zandy frowned. "I don't think I would like to see a
mine. I mean, my father has always told me what awful
places they are."

"We wouldn't have to go inside. I just thought it might
be nice to drive out to it. The day is starting to warm up,
and it looks like a perfect fall morning."

"We would drive?" Zandy questioned as she buttered

a slice of toast.

"That's another part of the surprise. I've bought a buggy and matched geldings for your use whenever you want to get around. It's quite a walk to the Mulvane house, and it would be much easier for you to go and visit if you had proper transportation," Riley replied.

"You bought a buggy for me?" Zandy questioned in surprise. "How very thoughtful! I would love to go for a ride with you. Can we go after breakfast?"

"I'd like that very much, Zandy."

Zandy hurried through breakfast and rushed to see her new gift. She thrilled to the feel of the fine leather upholstery in her new blue-and-gray buggy. The matched geldings were smoky gray with white boots, and Zandy nearly squealed with delight as Riley gave them a flick of the reins.

"Oh, this is so much fun," she said in an animated voice. She'd secured a pink bonnet on her head before climbing into the buggy, but now she wanted nothing more than to feel the wind through her hair.

Riley laughed as she pulled the hat off and took down her hair. Zandy ran her fingers through the long brown mass, freeing it to blow in the wind.

The drive to the Alexandra wasn't nearly as long as Zandy had hoped. She frowned slightly as Riley brought the horses to a stop.

"It doesn't look like much," Riley said with a shrug of his shoulders. "Mines usually don't look all that appealing."

"I've never cared for the way any of it looks. It's all so dark and depressing," Zandy said as she took Riley's offered hand. He helped her down from the buggy and showed her around the mine's entrance.

"Looks can be deceiving," Riley said as he lead Zandy to the entrance.

"I suppose," Zandy said apprehensively as she held back.

Riley grew acutely aware of his wife's fear. He dared to put his arm around her waist. "I didn't realize you were so afraid," he said as he pulled Zandy close.

"It's just all of the things my father has told me. The darkness and the feeling of being buried alive," Zandy said with a shudder.

Riley stopped and pulled Zandy around to face him. "I would never let anything happen to you. Do you trust me, even a little bit?"

Zandy lost herself in the darkness of Riley's eyes. "I, uh. . .," Zandy stammered as she grew increasingly aware of Riley's touch. "I trust you," she finally offered. Her mind reasoned that Riley had always been a man of his word.

"Then why not come inside with me? We can take a lantern, and it won't seem so dark. I promise to take care of you," Riley said in a husky whisper.

The wind blew Riley's hair into his eyes and, without thinking, Zandy reached up and pushed the hair away from his face. She found herself unable to take her hand away from his face and instead, allowed it to trail down his cheek to his dimpled chin.

For a moment, time stood still, and Zandy forgot the past and all that had marred their relationship.

Riley reached up to hold her hand against his face. "I think I could grow to like this," he whispered.

"Yes," Zandy murmured.

Riley continued to hold her hand as he bent down to kiss her. Zandy was soft and yielding in his arms and this time when she quivered, Riley realized with a start that Zandy trembled from pleasure and not revulsion. He wanted to give a yell, knowing that if Zandy could at least find herself attracted to him, then perhaps he could work through the other obstacles that kept them from having a real marriage.

Zandy's mind was a storm of confusion. She felt herself fall limp against her husband and a part of her wanted the moment to never end. Was she falling in love with Riley Dawson?

When Riley pulled away, Zandy blushed and lowered her face. It was hard enough to wonder what Riley expected of her as a wife, but these new feelings were completely unforeseen.

"Come on," Riley said as he stepped away to light the lantern. "We'll just go in a short ways. You might as well see what buys your bread and butter."

Zandy crushed little handfuls of her pink-and-white-striped skirt. She really didn't want to follow Riley into the black hole that presented itself before them but, if she said no, Riley would think that she didn't trust him.

Riley waited for her with the lantern in hand. He couldn't explain the feelings of protection that he felt for her. He watched her standing there. The turmoil on Zandy's face was evident, yet Riley silently hoped she'd have the courage to trust him. For some reason it suddenly seemed very important.

Zandy stepped forward slowly. "I'll go with you, but I can't lie and say that I'm not afraid."

"You aren't afraid of me, are you?" Riley asked, almost fearfully.

Zandy smiled up at her husband. "No, silly. The mine is what I'm afraid of," she said as she pointed to the entrance.

"Well, at least that's something," Riley said with a grin. "Come on."

Riley took hold of Zandy's arm and lead her into the mine. The air was stale even just a short way into the mine. Zandy wrinkled her nose and shivered at the dampness. She looked over her shoulder as Riley moved them farther down the tunnel. She cringed at the sight of the entryway growing smaller and smaller. There was little comfort in the fact that the lantern was their only light.

Zandy pushed close to Riley's body, grateful for his strong arm to lean on. "Riley, I don't like it in here. Do we have to go any farther?"

"I just want to show you where the main shaft is. This is where we lower the men and supplies deep into the ground. The best show of color is down below," Riley said as he held the lamp higher. "See, it's just over there."

Zandy strained to see in the dim light. They stood right at the edge of the shaft while Riley explained the headframe to Zandy. "This framework is set up to house the hoisting system that takes the men up and down. See, up there, is the sheave wheel. It's the pulley that holds the hoist cable." Riley held up the lantern so that Zandy could make out the contraption.

"It doesn't look very safe," Zandy said gravely. She remembered stories her father had told her of accidents where the cage that held the miners would suddenly plummet and kill everyone on board. Knowing that some shafts ran as deep as a hundred feet or more, Zandy backed away uncomfortably.

"There's always a risk," Riley agreed.

Zandy suddenly became aware of the sound of water. "I hear water. Is there an underground spring here?" Zandy questioned, eager to forget the shaft.

"There's always water in the mine. Pumping it out takes quite a bit of money. Come on, I'll show you what you're hearing," Riley said and pulled Zandy with him down a long, narrow tunnel.

"I don't like it here, Riley. Let's just go," Zandy said, tightening her grip on Riley's hand. "Please, Riley. I'm scared."

"Don't worry, Zandy," Riley said confidently. "I haven't gotten you hurt yet, and what I want to show you is just over here."

They rounded the corner, and Zandy was amazed to find a small pool of water with a steady stream of liquid dripping in from overhead. Further inspection showed that the water flowed away from the pool and trickled down rocks and black sand to disappear into the darkness.

Riley handed Zandy the lantern and went to the water and cupped some in his hand. "Here, taste. It's sweet and pure."

Zandy felt strange lowering her lips to Riley's hand but, nonetheless, she sampled the water. "It's very good."

Just then an ominous rumbling caught Zandy's ear. "Riley!"

"I hear it. We'd better get out of here," Riley said as he directed Zandy back to the tunnel.

The words were no sooner out of Riley's mouth than rock began to pour down around them, and dirt pelted Zandy's face.

"Alexandra, get back!" Riley pushed Zandy behind him just as the timber overhead gave way, and rock and debris came crashing down on top of him. Zandy had fallen backward and landed hard on the floor of the tunnel.

"Riley!" she screamed as the debris buried her husband.

Zandy sat fearfully, trying to protect the lantern. Without light the mine would truly become a stifling tomb. She thanked God that the rumbling stopped quickly, and everything quit shaking.

Shock seemed to stun her mind, but in a flash she knew that Riley had saved her life and was now buried in her place. Zandy turned up the lantern knowing that it would burn the precious kerosene even faster.

Taking account of the situation, Zandy realized Riley's death would present the perfect opportunity to free herself from his control. She knew that it would be simple to do nothing, but in her heart she couldn't. She set the lantern to one side and began to pull at the rocks and dirt with her hands.

The longer it took to dig out Riley's body, the more desperate Zandy became. "Please God, please help me save him. Don't let Riley die, I need him." The words startled Zandy, but she paid no attention to them.

Finally, Zandy was able to take hold of Riley's legs and pull him backwards and away from the rubble. She hurried to pull the lantern closer and noticed immediately that Riley was still breathing. "Oh, thank You, Father," she whispered.

Zandy brushed the hair away from Riley's face and was stunned to find her hand wet with blood when she pulled it back. Quickly, she tore strips from her petticoat and dipped them in the water to wash the wound.

Concern filled her heart as Zandy realized the ugly gash on Riley's head was quite deep. Blood continued to pour from it even as Zandy tried her best to stop the flow. "Help me, Father. He's dying. Please don't let him die," Zandy began to cry. She held pressure to the wound with one hand, as she worked feverishly to revive Riley with the other.

She bathed his face with the icy water and felt a bit of relief as Riley stirred. Even though he remained unconscious, Zandy was comforted to find that the bleeding had stopped.

The damp cold of the mine seemed to penetrate Zandy's bones and, after binding Riley's head, she worked to pull his body across her lap to keep him warm.

"Dear God," Zandy prayed as she looked around, "I need You so much. Please send someone to help us get out, and please save Riley." She hugged him close to her breast as a mother would a child. He didn't stir or make any further sound, and Zandy felt her heart grow heavy. Would God listen to her desperate plea?

sixteen

The dirt sifted and slithered around the weaken timbers as Zandy continued to cradle Riley's unconscious form. From time to time she heard rock break lose and fall, but at least it was a change in the monotonous sound of the water dripping and Riley's ragged breathing.

Zandy had turned the lantern down as low as it would go and leaned back again the damp, cold rock. As she held Riley, she gently stroked his face, hoping and praying that the stimulation would cause him to awaken.

She dozed off and on, more than a little aware of the poor air. She had thought to explore the direction of the stream, but she hated to leave Riley in his precarious state of life.

When she finally drifted off to sleep, Zandy was amazed that her dreams were peaceful and calming. She thought of Missouri in springtime and the sweet smell of apple blossoms as they filtered through her bedroom window from the orchard across the river.

Waking with a serenity that she'd not known in months, Zandy was startled to find Riley staring up at her.

"You're awake! Oh, praise God," Zandy said as she checked Riley's head.

"I figured I'd died, and you were an angel," he teased in a whisper.

"You didn't die, but very nearly. The mine buried you, and I thought you weren't breathing when I pulled you out."

"You saved me? Why?" Riley questioned weakly.

Zandy smiled, "I couldn't let you die."

"Why?" Riley persisted.

Zandy frowned slightly. What did he want her to say? "I'm not sure you'd understand," she finally said and added, "I'm not totally sure why except that you're one of God's creatures and He would expect no less of me."

"Oh," Riley said, sounding disappointed. "I suppose," he paused as if trying to gain a bit of strength, "I shouldn't question why, but just be grateful. Thank you."

"No thanks are necessary," Zandy said softly as she rested her hand against Riley's cheek. "I'm sure that you would have done the same for me."

"Of course I would," Riley murmured as his eyes fell closed. "But, then I love you."

Zandy was notably stunned, but her expression was of no concern for Riley because he'd already lost consciousness again. She dismissed the words in disbelief then tried to rationalize that his words were just those of a man afraid he was dying. Riley had wanted her for many reasons, but love was not one of them—at least she didn't have any reason to believe it was. Her moments of contemplation were few as Riley stirred to consciousness again.

"Alexandra," Riley moaned her name as he struggled to move.

"Lie still," Zandy commanded. "You've got a nasty

cut on your head, and you're going to start bleeding if you move."

Riley fell back against her. "I'm too heavy for you."

Zandy smiled. "Stop worrying about it and just relax."

"Tell me about your God, Alexandra."

The words shocked Zandy's senses. Riley was asking her to share God's love with him. He must feel confident that his life was coming to an end. It was often the common response of people who feared that death was shadowing their doorstep.

"Of course," Zandy said and breathed a silent prayer that she'd say the right thing. "I've never known a day in my life when God wasn't an important part of it. When my mother was still alive, I remember sitting on her lap and listening to her telling me stories about Jesus."

"Did you believe them?" Riley croaked the question. "The stories, that is. Did you think they were more than just stories?"

"Maybe not at first," Zandy said, trying to remember. "I was very little and listening to stories was a great way to pass an evening. My mother reminded me that I had heard people telling stories of things that had happened while I'd actually been present. She said that the stories of Jesus were true and had been handed down to us through the Bible, just like family stories are passed down."

"I've never read much of the Bible," Riley replied.

"I have," Zandy said as she reached over to turn up the lamp a bit. "It's a constant source of comfort to me.

It led the way for me to find Jesus as my personal Savior."

"And how did you do that?"

"Jesus told his disciples, as well as the people who came to hear Him speak, that they had to be born again. Of course one man, Nicodemus, couldn't help but think in literal terms, and he questioned Jesus as to how a person could become a baby and be born again. Jesus told him that people had to be born of flesh and spirit. When our mother gives life to us we are born of the flesh, but when Christ gives life to us we are born of the spirit for all eternity."

"And you really believe that Christ came to save us?" Riley asked, sounding almost hopeful.

"I certainly do. Jesus went on to tell Nicodemus that 'God so loved the world, that he gave his only begotten Son, that whosoever believeth in him should not perish, but have everlasting life.' That's from John, chapter three, verse sixteen."

"I can't imagine that God could overlook the kind of man I've been and save me just because I chose to believe that Jesus is the Son of God," Riley said in a groggy voice.

"Well, you need to repent of your sin as well," Zandy said and then added, "Romans, chapter six, verse twenty-three says, 'For the wages of sin is death; but the gift of God is eternal life through Jesus Christ our Lord.' We can't be close to God and live our lives away from His truth. It just can't be both ways."

"And God will really forgive us our sins?" Riley asked.

"Of course. The Bible says He will and I believe it."

"Why would God care so much, and how could He keep from blaming us later on for something we did, even if we ask Him to forgive us?" Riley blinked several times trying hard to stay awake.

"I can only tell you what the Bible says, Riley," Zandy said as she reached over and dipped a strip of cloth in the cool water. She moistened Riley's lips with the cloth and bathed his face in a loving manner. "Psalms is one of my favorite books of the Bible. Psalm 103 has several verses that I truly love. It says God is merciful and slow to anger. It also says, 'For as the heaven is high above the earth, so great is his mercy toward them that fear him. As far as the east is from the west, so far hath he removed our transgressions from us.' God lets the past be forgiven, and He doesn't hold it against us."

Riley fell silent as if contemplating Zandy's words. Zandy was growing cramped and uncomfortable against the hard rock wall. She tried to shift her weight and, when Riley didn't say anything, she realized that he was unconscious again.

Taking the opportunity to stretch, Zandy eased her body out from under Riley's and picked up the lantern. For the first time since she'd uncovered Riley, Zandy tried to survey the damage.

There was only the smallest opening at the top of the tunnel and the rest of the passage was buried in debris. Zandy sighed in relief knowing that at least a small amount of air was getting through to them.

She went back to where Riley lay sleeping and wished she could do more to make him comfortable. She knelt beside him and prayed. "Dear Father, You alone know that Riley and I are stuck in this mine. I'm asking You to send us help, Lord. We need to be rescued and soon, or Riley might die. Please God, don't let Riley die, I really need him to live. Amen."

Zandy got to her feet, unaware that Riley had opened his eyes. "For he shall give his angels charge over thee, to keep thee in all thy ways." Riley's remembrance of Psalm Ninety-one, verse eleven startled Zandy.

"I didn't know you were awake," Zandy whispered.

"I know. Sorry if I frightened you," Riley said as he worked his way up the wall to a sitting position. "I need to stay conscious, Zandy. I want you to help me stay awake."

Zandy nodded and reached down to tear away more of her petticoat. "I'll get these wet. They ought to help," Zandy said, trying to ignore the fact that Riley had overheard her praying.

She wet the cloth and came to where Riley sat propped against the wall. When she reached out to wipe his forehead, Riley caught her hand in his. "Thank you," he said as he focused his eyes on Zandy's worried face. "I don't deserve your kindness. . .nor God's, but I am grateful."

"You're welcome," Zandy said and her heart felt all aflutter. Riley's touch was the only warmth in the bone-chilling cold of the mine.

"Zandy," Riley said as he offered her a place beside him, "please sit here with me." Zandy nodded, grateful for the added warmth of Riley's body. "You're freezing," Riley said as he pulled her close.

"I know, but there doesn't seem to be anything to do about it," Zandy said, truly feeling the cold more than she had before.

"Well, you sit right here in my arms, and we will keep each other warm." Riley's free hand went to his head as a shot of pain nearly blinded him.

"Does it hurt a lot?" Zandy questioned.

"Not that much. I've certainly had worse," Riley said with a weak smile.

Zandy doubted that he was telling her the truth, but she didn't contradict him. Instead, she leaned against his chest enjoying the feeling that she was in God's care and Riley's arms.

"How long do you think it will take until someone realizes we're missing?" Zandy finally voiced the question that had been haunting her mind.

"Not long," Riley said confidently. "Mrs. Malloy will have a fit if we're not back by suppertime, which is," he paused to look at his pocket watch, "already an hour past."

"How will they find us?"

"Mrs. Malloy knows we were headed here. She'll send someone to check up on us and then—" Riley's words were cut short by the blast of the mine whistle. "There, see. We're well on our way to being rescued."

Zandy sat up and looked around. "But, Riley, we're pretty far into the mine. They'll be working forever to dig us out. It might take days, and I'm not sure we have days." The panic was clear in her voice.

"Don't you trust God to save you?" Riley asked as he fought to stay awake.

Zandy smiled. How like God to use Riley to reaffirm her faith! "Of course. I'm sorry. I must have sounded like a doubting Thomas."

Riley laughed. "Now that's one person I do remember from the Bible. I always saw myself in his place."

Zandy laughed but said nothing. She leaned back against Riley's open arm. It was hard to believe so many hours had passed since they'd first entered the mine and suddenly Zandy was starting to feel quite hungry.

"What would you have done," Riley finally asked, "if I hadn't forced you to marry me?"

The question surprised Zandy. She thought for a moment, staring out into the shadowy confines of her tomb. "I would have gone home to Missouri."

"You don't like it here?"

"No, it isn't really a matter of like or dislike of the place. I love the beauty here, but Missouri has its beauty, too. I just hate the mining life," she said and laughed. "Now I really hate it."

Riley laughed, too. "I guess I can understand that. What would you have done in Missouri?"

"I don't really know," Zandy answered honestly. "I've always had someone else taking care of me. If I had gone back to Missouri I'd have been on my own."

"You don't have any family back there?"

"No, and I don't figure I'll ever talk Pa into going back.
He loves the mountains," Zandy replied. "I do respect his dream, however. I know what it is to have dreams."

"And what are your dreams, Zandy?" Riley asked, suddenly very interested in what his wife had to say.

Zandy swallowed hard. She'd wanted to tell Riley how much she wanted their marriage to work. She wanted to explain that she had feelings for him that she'd not anticipated. But, where should she begin, and how could she explain her change of heart?

"This is rather difficult for me. I wanted to be courted and fall in love, marry, and have a family. I wanted to be a good mother like Ruth, and I wanted to grow old with my husband. I guess that sounds rather unambitious, but it was really all I ever wanted. Now, I'd just like to get out of here," Zandy said sadly.

She waited for Riley to say something and when he didn't, she sat up. "Riley?" He didn't answer her, and Zandy quickly felt his chest for proof of his deep, even breathing. "Oh, Riley, please wake up."

Time passed, and still Riley remained unconscious. Zandy was beginning to panic. She tried to wash his face with the cold water and, when that didn't help, she gently slapped at his cheek with the palm of her hand. Nothing.

"Oh, God," she cried, "please help him, Lord. He doesn't know You yet. Please don't let him die without salvation."

seventeen

Long into the night the town of Dawson worked at a feverish pitch to free Riley and Zandy from the mine. The cave-in was massive, and no one knew for sure which direction the couple had gone.

Mrs. Malloy was beside herself with grief, feeling that it was her fault that something hadn't been done sooner. Ruth Stewart went to the woman and assured her that she had done everything possible and now it was in God's hands. Mrs. Malloy nodded and agreed to pray with Ruth.

Hour after hour ticked by while the men dug and loaded dirt onto ore cars and dumped it over the side of a ravine. The efforts were slowed by the necessity to reinstall timber framing to support the newly cleared tunnels.

Work at the other mines halted, and shifts were organized to share the laborious task of digging out the Alexandra Mine. At dawn, several of the church ladies appeared and set up breakfast tables, while still more women appeared on an hourly basis and brought food and drink.

Zandy heard the sounds of workers and felt only a slight bit of encouragement. She called out over and over, but to no avail. Her voice simply couldn't carry through the length of the tunnel filled with debris.

She had tried to dig at her end of the tunnel but, without even the crudest instrument to work with, Zandy was forced to give up her efforts and conserve her rapidly fading strength. Finally in exhaustion, Zandy fell asleep beside Riley's unconscious form.

Mindless of the hours that past, Zandy felt weaker than ever when she awoke. The damp cold of the mine seemed slightly relieved by laying close to Riley, but it was then with much concern that Zandy realized that Riley's body was burning up.

Fever! Zandy checked the wound and found the telltale redness of proud flesh. Blood poisoning was setting in, and Zandy knew that brain fever would only be a short way behind that. Zandy looked around frantically for a way to stifle the poison that was spreading into Riley's system, but nothing revealed itself.

Zandy took the lantern and searched the area but found nothing. There weren't any herbs to work with and even a search of Riley's pockets failed to provide even a small amount of chewing tobacco which Zandy knew made a wonderful drawing poultice.

In dejected silence Zandy slipped to the floor and began to cry. She was cold and hungry and, while she tried to encourage herself with the fact that there was plenty of water, the stale air seemed only to further her depression and listlessness.

"How much longer, Lord?" she whispered into the dim light. She'd turned the lamp down hoping to conserve the precious kerosene as well as eliminate some of the smoke it put off.

She felt the tears begin to slide down her cheeks. "I've tried so hard to have faith, Father," she prayed as she cried. "I kept the faith through my ordeal when Riley insisted on my being his mistress, and I even stood fast to Your promises when there wasn't any food and the children were starving. Oh, Father, I know that You can make the way clear for the men to rescue us. I know You can save us. I put it all in Your hands, Lord. If I perish now, I know that I will wake up in Your house, and I don't fear death for myself." She paused and felt Riley's burning head. "I pray that he's made peace with You, Lord. I pray that You'll forgive Riley. I forgive him, Lord," she whispered. "I forgive him, and I love him." The words came naturally and had no startling revelation as Zandy presumed they would. *I really do love him*, she thought.

After two days of working to free Riley and Zandy, the men finally broke through the last few feet of debris to find the couple sleeping side by side, Zandy's arm placed protectively across her dying husband.

Riley's men were quick to carry the two outside, and while Zandy struggled to wake up, Riley remained gravely still.

"Take him up to the house," the doctor instructed, and K.C. and Pat loaded Riley into a nearby wagon and drove the team hard and fast to the Dawson mansion.

Burley Stewart knelt beside his barely conscious daughter. "Take her to our house," he instructed Tom and Jake Atkins.

Ruth had waited at the house for news of the rescue.

The boys remained subdued yet quietly argumentative with one another as they waited for news of their sister. Molly was an exceptionally good baby, and Ruth felt certain that she could sense the gravity of the household.

When the men came noisily up the walkway, Ruth clasped her hand to her throat. "Is she dead?" Ruth questioned as she ran to her husband's side.

"No, just exhausted and starved," Burley said in a concerned tone that told Ruth everything.

"Bring her in, she can have Joshua's bed," Ruth said as she led the way.

Zandy's dirt-caked body was placed upon the iron-framed bed. Tom and Jake offered their assistance if the Stewarts should need anything more, then took their leave.

Ruth began washing the dirt from her stepdaughter's body. "Burley, please put some more water on to boil, and Josh, you heat up some of that soup we had with lunch." Both nodded in agreement and went quickly from the room.

"How can I help?" George asked simultaneously with Bart and Samuel.

"You boys run and get one of my good nightdresses and the smelling salts."

The boys raced from the room, and Ruth peered down at the hopeless dress that Zandy wore. There was no way to repair the numerous tears. There would be ample enough money and time to get another, Ruth surmised and made the decision to cut the dress from Zandy's body.

She'd just finished cutting the gown from neck to hem

and covering Zandy with a blanket when the boys returned with the things she'd asked for. Ruth shooed them from the room and then went to work trying to revive Zandy.

Ruth waved the smelling salts under Zandy's nose until the weak fluttering of her stepdaughter's eyes gave her hope of Zandy's regaining consciousness.

"Alexandra, you wake up this minute," Ruth sounded gruff, hoping that it would bring Zandy around faster.

"Where am I?" Zandy whispered from a raspy throat.

"You're safe with us at the Mulvane house," Ruth said softly.

"Where. . .?" her words faded as she fought to stay awake. "Where is Riley?"

"He's with the doctor. You have to rest here and get some food in you before you can see him," Ruth said firmly.

"Have. . .to. . .have to see. . .him," Zandy insisted.

"No, darling," Burley said as he brought fresh water in for Ruth to use. "You can't see him just yet. You've got to get your strength back."

"Oh, Pa," Zandy began to cry although she had no strength for it. "Don't let him die."

Ruth and Burley exchanged brief worried looks before trying to minister to their daughter's needs. Zandy could only stay awake long enough to take in a small amount of soup and, after Ruth finished bathing her, she got Zandy dressed and settled into bed for a much-needed rest.

Ruth remained by Zandy's side constantly, and whenever her stepdaughter opened her eyes even for a brief moment, Ruth managed to get some warm soup or beef broth down her throat. There wasn't a moment when Ruth wasn't in a state of prayer, nor when she didn't ponder the anxiety and concern in Zandy's plea to keep Riley from dying. Was it possible that love had come to Zandy in such a short time?

After three days of tumultuous sleep, Zandy managed to feel rested. An exhausted Ruth eased pillows behind her stepdaughter's back and helped her to sit up.

"I feel like I could eat a horse," Zandy said weakly.

"That's a good sign," Ruth said in a joyous voice. "I'll fix you whatever you like. We have a full larder. What will you have?"

"Anything and everything," Zandy replied and then changed her mind. "No, I want to see Riley. How is he?" she threw back the covers and struggled to sit up.

"You can't just jump up out of bed after all that you've been through. I'm sure Riley is fine. I haven't heard anything all day, but your pa has tried to keep apprised of the situation. I'm sure he'll tell us whatever he knows when he comes home from work."

"But I have to know," Zandy stated firmly. "Couldn't we send one of the boys?"

"They're all in school, Zandy. You'll just have to wait until three o'clock. That's only two hours away, and your pa will be back shortly after that."

Zandy nodded and eased back into the pillows. "How long did I sleep?" she questioned as she pulled the covers back.

"This is the third day."

"No!" Zandy exclaimed. "I don't believe it. How could I have slept all that time? Now I really have to find out about Riley."

Ruth put her hand out to stop her stepdaughter. "You haven't the strength to even dress. Now, do as you are told. I promise I'll send someone up to the Dawson mansion, if you'll promise to stay put until I get back."

Zandy nodded. "I will. I promise. Just please hurry." Zandy said in a pleading tone that spurred Ruth on.

Ruth had pulled on her coat and was just about to leave the house when Burley appeared on the walkway. The prematurity of his arrival told Ruth instantly that he would not be the bearer of good news.

"Is it Riley?" she asked fearfully as her husband approached the porch.

"Yes," Burley whispered. "He's dead."

Ruth swayed back against the porch rail. "Dead? Are you sure?"

"The doctor came and told me just a few minutes ago."

"Oh, my poor Alexandra. This will not be easy," Ruth said with tears in her eyes.

"I want to tell her," Burley said firmly and walked passed his wife and into the house.

After several minutes, Ruth could hear Zandy's ragged sobs and went to join Burley in trying to offer consolation to their daughter.

The days that followed passed in a blur for Zandy Dawson. People told her that that was God's way of easing her burden. She performed her duties mechanically, issuing instructions for the funeral, with her father's help. There was nothing comforting about burying a husband. Especially one whose salvation remained a burning question in Zandy's mind. *Had Riley found the Lord before he died?*

Too stunned to cry, Zandy went through the motions of attending the largest funeral she'd ever known. Hundreds of people turned out to bid their respects to the closed casket of Riley Dawson. When it was all over, Zandy returned to the mansion alone, despite her father's insistence that she come home with her family.

She moved through the house in her widow's weeds, touching the things that reminded her of Riley and, when nothing offered any real consolation, she went to his old bedroom and sat for hours in his desk chair.

Looking down at the desk, Zandy started turning the pages of the ledgers that showed the percentages of profits and losses that Riley had recorded for each and every business transaction in town. When she finally came upon his bank ledgers, she gasped. Riley Dawson was a millionaire.

"No," she thought aloud, "I am."

A plan immediately formed in her mind to release the townspeople from their debt to Riley. She made out notices for immediate posting and called a town meeting of the business owners.

Within a week, the town of Dawson was singing the praises of their dead mayor's widow. At first everyone had been stunned to learn of Zandy's plan, but they eagerly accepted her generosity.

Zandy knew that she was doing the right thing, but it

offered her very little relief from the emptiness. Zandy was greatly relieved when Burley and Ruth showed up to offer a hand with anything she might need.

"I'm so happy to see you," Zandy said as she rang for Mrs. Malloy. The older woman appeared almost instantly.

"Yes, Mrs. Dawson?"

"Please bring us some refreshments," Zandy said as she took a seat across from her parents.

"Certainly," Mrs. Malloy replied and was gone.

"You really don't have to give us refreshments, Zandy. We just stopped by to see if we could help you," Ruth said as she reached out to pat Zandy's hand.

"I've been thinking a great deal since Riley. . .," Zandy fell silent. "Since he died," she finally said. "I asked the doctor if Riley accepted Christ, but he didn't know." Zandy felt her eyes fill with tears. "It's really all that I wanted for him. I wanted him to understand that life without God was already a way of being dead."

"Did you share the Gospel with him, Zandy?" Burley asked his daughter gently.

"Yes, when he was dying. But," Zandy paused as she wiped her cheeks, "I don't know if he was conscious enough to understand what I was telling him or not. I pray that he accepted God, but I just don't know." Zandy put her face in her hands and began to sob.

"Alexandra," Burley began as he knelt down beside his daughter, "you must trust God and place your worries in His hands. Whether you sit here and worry, spending hours in tears and grief or not, ultimately God is still sovereign and still in control. Leave it with Him,

Zandy, and let your life go on. You lived your Christianity in front of him, despite what he wanted you to do."

Zandy's head snapped up. "What do you mean?" she questioned, suddenly sober.

Burley leaned back on his heel. "I know that he expected you to be his mistress and not his wife."

"How?"

"You were delirious. You told it all," Burley explained. "When I realized what I had pushed you to do, I couldn't forgive myself."

"Your father's pain was so great," Ruth added, "that he cried for hours. He just kept saying—"

"It isn't important," Burley interrupted. "What is important is that God was watching over you, even when I wasn't. You've got to trust Him now."

Zandy nodded. "I know you're right."

"What will you do now?" Ruth questioned softly.

"I want to go home, to Missouri," Zandy said firmly. "I have more than enough money to take all of us home in style. Please say you'll come back to Missouri with me. I'll pay for everything, and we'll still have plenty to buy the biggest store you'd ever want. Please say yes."

Burley looked into the pleading eyes of his daughter. "I can't, Alexandra. We've made this our home," Burley said, looking across the small space to his wife.

Ruth nodded in agreement. "We belong here, Zandy."

"Well, at least move into the mansion," Zandy begged. "I'm going back to Missouri, but this big house needn't stand empty. There's a house full of staff that need to maintain their jobs. I have more than enough money to maintain the estate and all the staff for as long as you want them. Please, let me do this for you."

"No," Burley said, shaking his head. "I can't take charity from my daughter."

"Then don't let it be charity. Take over the estate and holdings for me and be my manager. You can have any salary you wish, this house, staff, and full control. I'll need someone honest to look out for my interests."

"She's got a point, Burley. The lawlessness of this town would take advantage of a vulnerable young widow."

"All right," Burley agreed. "I'll do it."

A week later, Zandy took one final walk through the house. She had a large bank draft, more than enough to take care of her needs for a long time. There was really nothing left to hold her here, and yet she felt reluctant to let go of Riley's memory.

She went to his bedroom in search of their wedding picture but, when she couldn't find it, she settled instead for a tintype of Riley that had been taken a year or two before Zandy had met him. He was smiling that self-assured smile that had always appeared smug and demanding. Zandy clutched the photo to her breast. "Oh, Riley."

Mrs. Malloy announced from the hall that her parents had arrived to take her to the stage.

"I'm coming," Zandy called and tucked the picture into her coat pocket. Turning to face the room for one last time, Zandy smiled. "What time I am afraid, I will trust in thee," she murmured the words of Psalm 56:3.

eighteen

The fall of 1881 found southern Missouri in a riot of autumn color. Zandy Dawson stood on the front porch of her boardinghouse and breathed deeply of the glorious scents. The last roses of summer persevered to hang onto the white painted trellis at the end of the porch. Their sweet, muted aroma lingered in the morning air and mingled with the smell of fresh coffee and bacon.

Zandy pulled a watch from her pocket and realized that it would be only a matter of minutes before the breakfast crowd would be storming down her stairs and across her parlor to the dining room.

She thought for a moment to go inside and assist Ann, her hired help, with the breakfast but knew the woman would resent any offer. Ann prided herself in keeping the house in perfect order and even managed the new guests for Zandy. Zandy only had to keep the books and tend to the shopping, which Ann hated with a passion.

Life in Missouri had been rewarding and refreshing, and inwardly Zandy knew that she'd made the right decision to come back. Although she'd settled far from her hometown, Zandy was content with her choice. In fact, it was hard to believe that a whole year had passed since she'd left Colorado.

The boardinghouse was huge and brought in a reasonable profit, although from the newest ledger report from her father, Zandy knew that she didn't need the money.

She found ways to use it, however, contributing heavily to the church and orphanage.

Zandy smoothed down the red-sprigged calico bodice and resecured the ties of her apron. While she'd kept the name Dawson, she'd discarded her widow's weeds after reaching Denver. She had deliberated long and hard about the decision and finally concluded that she would not present herself as a widow.

Rational reasoning told her that she'd have enough to explain to people by simply being a new face in town. Then, should she ever decide to remarry, though she'd firmly decided she wouldn't, Zandy knew it would be difficult to explain having been a bride without having consummated her marriage.

And the proposals had come, just as Zandy presumed they would. Not because she was a raving beauty, but more so because she was financially affluent and news like that simply couldn't be contained. One could not just ignore a bank account with several thousand dollars in it and seemingly no end in sight of those funds being diminished.

Zandy leaned against the porch post and sighed. Remarrying was not for her. She hadn't realized how much she loved Riley until he was dead. She felt the tears slide down her cheeks as they often had during the last year.

There was no forgetting the husband about whom she had known so little. Logic concluded that she would simply be Alexandra Dawson, the new boardinghouse owner, and, while people might talk about a single woman running such an establishment, Zandy didn't care. She was as happy as she could be and only during peaceful, quiet moments like this did she acknowledge the emptiness in her heart.

At the sound of voices in the house, Zandy knew that it was time was breakfast. She went in and took her place at the table, offering grace and helping Ann see to everyone's needs.

Later in the day, Zandy took Ann's list of groceries and headed into town to pick up the laundry and do the household shopping.

The town was bustling, and one of the largest that Zandy had ever lived in. She gingerly stepped into the street and narrowly missed a freighter as it went streaking around the corner from a side street. Zandy clung tightly to her basket, steadied her nerves, and went on about her business. It was just another day.

On her way home, Zandy stopped by the house of her seamstress and picked up the new gown she had ordered some weeks earlier.

"Mighty good to see you, Zandy. Can you sit a spell and have some cake and coffee?"

"Sorry, no," Zandy told the older woman. "Although I must say it is hard to pass up a chance to eat your cake."

"I'll just pack some for you to take home," the white-haired woman smiled.

Zandy smiled and waited while the woman wrapped two pieces of lemon cake in a tea towel. Zandy placed them in her already crowded basket and bid the woman good day.

As Zandy moved down the street of white picket fences and huge cottonwood trees, she felt as though she was being watched. Turning abruptly to glance behind her, Zandy found nothing to indicate her concern. Nonetheless, she picked up her pace and hurried to the safety of home.

Ann chided her when she relayed her concerns. "You should take a buggy or ride one of the horses. It isn't safe for you to walk all that way alone."

"But I like to walk. The day is probably one of the last warm ones we'll have," Zandy argued. "I didn't have any problem. I just said that I felt like someone was watching me."

Ann, who acted like Zandy's senior but in fact was a year younger, sniffed in disgust and, after taking her slice of lemon cake, retired to the kitchen to finish baking.

Zandy shook her head and went to her own quarters. Two rooms at the back of the house with a large enclosed porch, were Zandy's domain. The privacy afforded her here was both a refuge and a bittersweet reminder of all that she'd lost.

She put the cake on a table and then carefully unwrapped the new dress. Lovingly, she spread the blue gown on her bed. This would be a dress reserved for Sundays and special occasions, she'd decided. The princess style gown sported many gores with tight-fitting steels placed in the waist to show off Zandy's slender form. The dress was cut low and made without sleeves in order to be worn with a white shirtwaist. This would allow her to make it either a very elegant affair with a silk and lace blouse, or a more simple one out of plain cotton.

The noise of a wagon in the front yard caused Zandy to stop daydreaming. She went in search of Ann and found her already preparing to check in new boarders. Zandy knew this was the routine as her boardinghouse was the best in town, and though outside of the main city proper, it was always crowded with both short- and long-term customers.

Proud that her reputation for cleanliness and good food had spread all the way to Kansas City, Zandy scarcely ever found the house less than half full.

She stayed behind the scenes lest she offend Ann by trying to crowd her. The new boarders, three women and two men, were capably handled by Ann, and soon they were cleared from the entryway and directed to their rooms upstairs. Zandy was about to go to the kitchen for a bite of lunch when a third man caught her eye as he entered into the foyer.

The bearded man was covered in dust and had his hat pulled low. He walked with a slow, deliberate stride to the desk where Ann offered him a pen to register. Something about him seemed vaguely familiar and Zandy tried to place him, wondering suddenly if it was someone she'd known in Colorado.

As soon as the man had registered and gone upstairs, Zandy hurried to the desk and turned the register book around to read the name.

The only mark given was an *X* where a name would have normally been signed. Zandy sighed. Perhaps she'd be able to find out something more later.

Still in turmoil at suppertime, Zandy asked Ann to bring a tray to her room and to lead the boarders in grace. Ann nodded and was so quick with her work that Zandy had scarcely taken a seat when Ann appeared with her dinner.

"Thanks, Ann. I truly appreciate this," Zandy said, knowing that Ann hated it when a boarder would take a meal in his room.

Ann nodded, then quickly pulled the door shut and retreated down the hall. Zandy took the tray with her to the enclosed porch and sat down to enjoy the sunset.

The sky looked as if it were ablaze. The flaming orange sun seemed to catch the horizon on fire with ruby streaks bursting out across the blue-and-gold sky.

With a sigh, Zandy reached out to take hold of Riley's picture. She traced the edge of the frame and wondered silently if Riley were in Heaven. Tears fell again as Zandy realized it had been nearly a year to the day since Riley had died. Hearing the door open behind her, Zandy knew it would be Ann checking to see if she needed anything.

Not wanting Ann to see her crying, Zandy struggled to control her voice. "I don't need anything, Ann. I'll bring the tray to the kitchen when I'm done."

At the sound of the door's closing, Zandy leaned back against the wicker chair. She felt the loneliness like a twisting knife in her soul. It wasn't good for her to continue pondering Riley's death, but it seemed impossible to get past it. Maybe Ann was right. Maybe what she needed was a good strong man to help her spend her money. She laughed out loud—her money indeed! "Hello, Alexandra."

The rich baritone of a man's voice rang out and Zandy thought she must be going mad. She did nothing for a moment until the man came to stand beside her. Fearing the end result, Zandy slowly raised her gaze to find that the face did indeed match the voice.

"Riley!" Zandy jumped to her feet and threw herself into her husband's arms. She covered his clean-shaven face with kisses, while tears fell down her face leaving their salty wetness on Riley's face.

"Whoa," Riley said as he set Zandy away from him. "I certainly didn't expect a response like this or I'd have come a lot sooner."

Zandy clutched her hand to her throat suddenly fearing that she'd faint. "You. . .you were the man in the lobby. I knew you looked familiar." She gasped for air, feeling the darkness of unconsciousness trying to claim her.

"Here," Riley instructed, "sit down, and I'll get you some water."

"No!" Zandy said and grabbed Riley's arm tightly. "Don't leave me. If this is a dream, I'm not ready to give it up yet."

Riley knelt beside her, touching her wet cheeks gently. "It's no dream, Alexandra. I'm really here."

"You can't be. I must be mad," Zandy said sadly and leaned back hard against the chair.

"You aren't mad," Riley grinned, "just the most beautiful woman I've ever known. You look even prettier than the day we were married."

Zandy dropped her hold, but said nothing. She simply couldn't believe that her husband had come back from the dead. Before she could say a word, Riley pulled up a chair and sat directly in front of her.

"I'm sorry this is such a shock. I had to come and tell you that I've accepted Christ as my Savior. I did in fact accept Him that day in the mine when you told me about Him."

Zandy stared, dumbfounded. Was this some form of kindness from the Lord to let her know that Riley was safely in Heaven? She'd wondered for so long, fearful that he'd never received salvation, that perhaps her mind was failing her.

"Did you hear me, Alexandra?" Riley asked as he took hold of her hands.

His touch felt real enough, Zandy thought as she looked first to her hands and then to his face. "What?" she finally questioned.

"I've come to ask your forgiveness. I know how much I wronged you. I've dealt with everything else in my life," Riley said and then added, "everything but you."

"Forgive you?" Zandy heard her voice ask, but the words sounded as if they belonged to someone else. "I forgave you a long time ago. I prayed that you'd come to know Christ, and my only hope was that you'd find salvation before you died."

Riley smiled. "I did. Thanks to you and your perseverance. God knew what He was doing when He sent you into my life."

Zandy suddenly realized that it was all real. Riley was alive and sitting on her back porch, holding her hands. She didn't know whether to cry anew or laugh.

"Why?" was the only word Zandy could manage for a moment. She took her hands from Riley's and reached out to touch his face. "Why did you let me believe you were dead?"

nineteen

Riley sat silently, staring into Zandy's eyes. How could he explain everything that he'd gone through? The weeks of recuperation stood out in his mind, and so he began the detailed explanation.

"I regained consciousness when Doc had me taken to the mansion. I told him that I wanted him to get me away from Dawson and tell everyone I'd died. I couldn't deal with my feelings, Zandy. I'm sorry," Riley offered the words as a humble apology.

"I still don't understand. It hurt so much when they told me you were dead. A part of me died, too. It was like having my heart ripped out."

"I had no idea you'd feel that way," Riley admitted. "I figured you'd be relieved. I thought I'd forced you into a loveless marriage because of my lustful intentions. The night of our wedding I knew I'd fallen in love with you and I hated myself."

"For falling in love with me?" Zandy questioned trying hard to hide her surprise at Riley's declaration of love.

"No," Riley said taking her hands from his face. "For taking you as my wife. . .without a willing heart. I couldn't stay with you and make matters worse." Riley's words were whispers. "Although, walking away from you was the hardest thing I've ever done."

Zandy stared at him with a puzzled frown. "You deliberately chose not to consummate our marriage?"

"Can you imagine it any other way?" Riley said with a laugh. "I was used to taking whatever I wanted. Wild horses couldn't have stopped me, but God wouldn't let me defile you."

"But we were married, and I had agreed to whatever that meant," Zandy said boldly.

"I know, but you were still forced. You had no other way out. I'd created an awful situation for you and made myself your only savior."

"That's where you're wrong, Riley. I had the only Savior I needed. I had Jesus, and there was nothing else that could change that. I agreed to marry you because it seemed the logical thing to do."

"Exactly my point," Riley sighed. "You didn't marry me for love, except maybe the love of your folks and siblings. I just couldn't live with myself, knowing that I'd forced you to marry a man that you didn't love and probably never would."

"I've thought about you every day since the accident," Zandy said. "I was so stunned when they told me you were dead, nothing seemed right from that moment on. People kept telling me I'd feel better, but I didn't. I went through your papers, made all the changes I thought necessary, and begged my family to return to Missouri with me. When they refused, I made the decision to go it alone," Zandy relayed the information knowing full well that Riley would have already learned all of this on his own.

Riley nodded. "I know. I kept up on your whereabouts through Doc. Zandy, please understand I needed to straighten out my life. I'd made a lot of mistakes and when I accepted Christ, I knew I could no longer ignore those mistakes. I saved dealing with you until last, because you are the most important. I didn't want you to think that I was just telling you what you wanted to hear by declaring my salvation in Christ, or for that matter, my love for you."

The second reference to love was too much for Zandy. "You love me?" Somehow that was harder to believe than the fact that Riley had come to know the Lord, though both thoughts thrilled Zandy's heart.

"I think I have loved you from the moment I first saw you wrestling those wild brothers of yours. I walked in expecting to take the town of Temperance for all it was worth. I planned to wring it dry, force everyone to become so dependent upon me that without me they'd be forced to leave. The power seemed so important to me, until I suddenly found something that I couldn't overpower—you," Riley said honestly.

"And you're certain that what you feel is love and not just guilt?" Zandy asked bluntly.

Riley studied her soft face for a moment. She'd pinned up her hair loosely so that wisps of hair fell in a frame around her face, and her green eyes were so intense and dark that Riley could forget his very purpose if he stared too long.

"I know it's love. You are my wife, Zandy," Riley said as he got to his feet and pulled Zandy up with him. "Is there any way you could find it in your heart to accept me as your husband? I don't mean right away. I wouldn't ask that much of you. But maybe in time, after we courted for a while, then maybe we could remarry."

"No," Zandy said firmly as she put her arms around Riley's neck. "I don't want to court my husband. I have a willing heart to be your wife, Riley Dawson, and I have no intention of waiting weeks, maybe even months, until you go through the motions of making me your wife. You accept your responsibilities now, or leave for good." Zandy stated firmly, but with a twinkle in her eye. She knew full well what Riley's response would be.

Riley crushed Zandy to him and lowered his lips to passionately cover hers. He kissed her with a longing that crossed the miles and months since he'd last seen her. "Wife," he breathed the word. "My beautiful, beautiful Christian wife."

Zandy put her head on Riley's chest and sighed. "I knew God would give me the desires of my heart."

Riley wrapped his arms tightly around Zandy. "I praise God for giving you a strong faith. If you hadn't stood by your convictions and God's principles, I would have ruined us both. God is truly good to have provided me with a woman of strong Biblical courage."

Zandy smiled to herself. God truly was good, and His mercies were everlasting. This He'd proven to Zandy more than once. Now He'd rewarded her trust by leading Riley to salvation.

"I love you, Alexandra Dawson," Riley said with as much love as Zandy had ever heard in a man's voice.

"And I love you, Riley Dawson," she breathed the words, "with all my willing heart."

A Letter To Our Readers

Dear Reader:

In order that we might better contribute to your reading enjoyment, we would appreciate your taking a few minutes to respond to the following questions. When completed, please return to the following:

Rebecca Germany, Editor
Heartsong Presents
P.O. Box 719
Uhrichsville, Ohio 44683

1. Did you enjoy reading *The Willing Heart*?
   ☐ Very much. I would like to see more books
      by this author!
   ☐ Moderately
      I would have enjoyed it more if _____

   _____

2. Are you a member of *Heartsong Presents*? Yes   No
   If no, where did you purchase this book? _____

   _____

3. What influenced your decision to purchase
   this book? (Circle those that apply.)

Cover	Back cover copy
Title	Friends
Publicity	Other _____

4. On a scale from 1 (poor) to 10 (superior), please rate the following elements.

___Heroine   ___Plot

___Hero   ___Inspirational theme

___Setting   ___Secondary characters

5. What settings would you like to see covered in *Heartsong Presents* books?

_____

_____

6. What are some inspirational themes you would like to see treated in future books?_____

_____

_____

7. Would you be interested in reading other *Heartsong Presents* titles?   Yes   No

8. Please circle your age range:

Under 18   18-24   25-34
35-45   46-55   Over 55

9. How many hours per week do you read? _____

Name _____

Occupation _____

Address _____

City _____ State _____ Zip _____

·········Presents·········

Great Inspirational Romance at a Great Price!

Heartsong Presents books are inspirational romances in contemporary and historical settings, designed to give you an enjoyable, spirit-lifting reading experience. You can choose from 60 wonderfully written titles from some of today's best authors like Lauraine Snelling, Brenda Bancroft, Sara Mitchell, and many others.

When ordering quantities less than twelve, above titles are $2.95 each.

LOVE A GREAT LOVE STORY?

Introducing Heartsong Presents —
Your Inspirational Book Club

Heartsong Presents Christian romance reader's service will provide you with four never before published romance titles every month! In fact, your books will be mailed to you at the same time advance copies are sent to book reviewers. You'll preview each of these new and unabridged books before they are released to the general public.

These books are filled with the kind of stories you have been longing for—stories of courtship, chivalry, honor, and virtue. Strong characters and riveting plot lines will make you want to read on and on. Romance is not dead, and each of these romantic tales will remind you that Christian faith is still the vital ingredient in an intimate relationship filled with true love and honest devotion.

Sign up today to receive your first set. Send no money now. We'll bill you only $9.97 post-paid with your shipment. Then every month you'll automatically receive the latest four "hot off the press" titles for the same low post-paid price of $9.97. That's a savings of 50% off the $4.95 cover price. When you consider the exaggerated shipping charges of other book clubs, your savings are even greater!

THERE IS NO RISK—you may cancel at any time without obligation. And if you aren't completely satisfied with any selection, return it for an immediate refund.

TO JOIN, just complete the coupon below, mail it today, and get ready for hours of wholesome entertainment.

Now you can curl up, relax, and enjoy some great reading full of the warmhearted spirit of romance.